The Secret
of the
Desert Stone

The Cooper Kids Adventure Series®

The Secret of the Desert Stone

Frank E. Peretti

WORD PUBLISHING
Dallas·London·Vancouver·Melbourne

Unless otherwise indicated, Scripture quotations are from the *International Children's Bible, New Century Version,* copyright © 1983, 1986, 1988.

Managing Editor: Laura Minchew
Project Editor: Beverly Phillips

Library of Congress Cataloging-in-Publication Data

Peretti, Frank E.
     The secret of the desert Stone / Frank E. Peretti.
         p.   cm. — (The Cooper Kids Adventure Series® ; 5)

     Summary: Fourteen-year-old Jay and his younger sister Lila accompany their father to the tiny African nation of Togwana where they experience a supernatural phenomenon through a mysterious stone.
     ISBN 0-8499-3643-8
     [1. Supernatural—Fiction. 2. Christian life—Fiction. 3. Africa—Religion—Fiction.] I. Title. II. Series: Peretti, Frank E. The Cooper Kids Adventure Series® ; 5.
PZ7.P4254Se   1996
[Fic]—dc20   96–1919
                                                                                        CIP
                                                                                        AC

Printed in the United States of America

97 98 99 00 RRD 9 8 7

ONE

The sky was still black, the stars were still out, and dawn was nothing more than a thin, red ribbon along the horizon when the sirens went off, wailing rudely across the vast army camp. As one man, the army of black warriors awoke—there were no dawdlers, no one who dared to slumber beyond reveille. The desert rattled with the slap and clatter of a thousand hands grabbing a thousand rifles. The soldiers leaped to their feet and burst from their tents, dashing across the sand, lining up in long, even rows on the flat desert. They stood at attention, rifles ready, eyes straight ahead, primed for battle.

Field Marshal Idi Nkromo was already awake and strutting about at the front of the camp, watching his army come to life. He was a heavy-set, marble-eyed man with medals and ribbons adorning his chest—most were of his own design, and most he had awarded himself. He scowled; he glared; he growled orders to his lieutenants, his hand always on the gleaming saber that hung at his side.

He nodded approvingly to himself. Yes, this would

be the moment, the final engagement, the ultimate display of his power. After this day, his rule over the tiny African nation of Togwana would be complete and absolute. After this campaign across the desert, no one would dare to . . . he became distracted by a muttering, a buzzing among the troops. Nkromo was displeased. Why were they not all standing rigid and silent? Hadn't enough soldiers been beaten or shot to enforce discipline? The light of dawn was just now revealing their faces, and they were staring anxiously toward the desert, exchanging worried glances with each other and whispering through the ranks.

Nkromo drew his saber and bellowed, "Order!"

The soldiers stiffened at attention, but there was still a stirring, and their faces held wide-eyed fear.

"Mobutu!"

"Sir!" Mobutu, a younger, thinner man in a khaki uniform, came on the run.

Nkromo pointed his saber at his army. "Find out who's causing this disturbance and drag them out to be shot!"

Mobutu didn't respond.

Nkromo shot a deadly glare his way, but Mobutu wasn't looking at him. The thin lieutenant and chief secretary was looking toward the desert—the same direction the army was looking. He appeared stunned, his mouth hanging open, his eyes wide with horror.

"Mobutu!"

Mobutu pointed toward the desert. "Sir . . . if you would look . . ."

Nkromo never took advice. "Mobutu, maintain

order in the ranks." Then, as if it were his idea, he added, "I think I'd like to survey the desert."

Nkromo turned with a deliberate casualness and looked across the barren expanse rimmed on the north and south by towering, rocky crags, just becoming visible in the light of dawn.

The saber fell from his trembling hand and clattered on the stones and sand.

THUNK! Jay Cooper, fourteen, strong, wiry, and sweating in the sun, swung a sledgehammer and drove the last wooden stake into the ground. Then he wound the end of a heavy rope around it and tightened it down with a few more whacks from the hammer. He had driven several stakes to hold the ropes tied around the base of a huge stone pillar etched with ancient relief carvings, hieroglyphics, and, near the top, the faces of Greek gods. The pillar was massive, at least three feet thick and thirty feet tall. It stood in the center of a vast excavation, the unearthing of what used to be an ancient Greek temple on a high bluff over the Mediterranean.

Dangling like an acrobat by a rope and harness, Dr. Jacob Cooper struggled to tighten a loop of cable around the crown of the pillar, being careful not to mar the chiseled face of the Greek god Zeus. "Okay, Lila," he called, "more slack."

Lila Cooper, thirteen, was perched on the ancient temple wall, her eyes alert and her long blond hair tied back for safety. She was operating a sizable gas-powered winch and feeding more cable to her father.

This precarious perch was making her a bit nervous. The excavated floor of the old temple wasn't that far down, only twelve feet or so, but just outside the wall she sat on was a steep cliff dropping several hundred feet to the sea. She could see the barge from the museum floating close to the shore, ready for loading; it was almost eighty feet long, but from up here it was the size of a postage stamp. She tried not to look that direction and pushed the lever to release more cable.

Dr. Cooper edged his way around the face of Zeus like a skilled rock climber, his muscular arms groping for any handhold he could find. When he finally got the cable secure just above Zeus's head, he exhaled a sigh of relief. "Okay, tighten her up."

Lila pulled the lever and the big drum of the winch turned, winding in the cable until it was tight.

Dr. Cooper climbed to the very top of the pillar and sat there like a seagull atop a flagpole. He removed his wide-brimmed hat and brushed back his blond hair, now slick with sweat. Looking thirty feet straight down, he could see his son, Jay, had the bottom of the pillar staked and secured with ropes so it wouldn't kick out when they tipped it over; looking toward the sea he saw his daughter, Lila, on the temple wall, ready to start lowering the pillar with the main winch. On the other side of the temple, Dr. Cooper's two crewmen, Bill and Jeff, were just getting ready to ease a long, flatbed trailer down a dirt ramp to the base of the pillar.

"So far so good," Dr. Cooper said to himself.

The plan was to secure a few more cables to the

pillar, carefully lower it onto the trailer, and then haul it down an access road to the sea. A crew was already waiting there to load the pillar onto a barge and transport it to the Museum of Antiquities in Athens. Barring any disasters, Jacob Cooper and his crew might finish this project today.

Dr. Cooper waved at Bill and Jeff and called, "All right, bring the trailer down."

Bill, a big, mustached man with a southern drawl, climbed into the cab of the old diesel truck while Jeff, limber and usually nervous, stood on the dirt ramp below to give hand signals. The starter growled, then the engine rumbled to life, black smoke bursting from the old stacks above the cab.

Jeff waved and called, "Okay, ease her back . . ."

Bill ground the old beast into reverse and slowly let out the clutch. The truck and trailer started inching down the steep dirt ramp toward the base of the pillar.

Dr. Cooper watched their progress from his lofty perch. The dirt ramp seemed to be working okay although it might be a little steep for that old rig. "Hey . . ." he started to say, "slow up, you're—"

"You're going too fast!" Jeff hollered.

Bill stomped on the brake pedal. Something snapped and the pedal went clear to the floor. The trailer started rolling down the ramp, picking up speed, pulling the truck backward.

"Slow up!" Jeff yelled. He jumped out of the way, rolling in the dirt, as the trailer rumbled and bounced right past him.

Bill tried to pull on the parking brake. It broke

off. He killed the ignition. The ramp was too steep, the trailer too heavy. The truck only slid backward down the incline, its rear tires slipping, growling over the dirt.

The flatbed was heading right for the base of the pillar.

Jay ran to get clear and hollered, "Dad!"

Dr. Cooper could see it coming: a big disaster. Maybe they *wouldn't* finish this project today.

CRUNCH! The trailer crashed into the pillar. Dr. Cooper could feel the pillar quiver under him.

Then he could feel it moving. The cable from Lila's winch went slack.

The pillar was falling right toward Lila!

"Look out!" her father yelled, holding on for dear life.

Lila screamed and dashed along the wall to get clear. Jay scrambled to safety as the base of the pillar began to tear loose. *PING! POP!* The heavy ropes plucked the stakes from the ground like rotten teeth.

The pillar picked up speed, falling like a big tree. Wind whistled by Dr. Cooper's head, and his hat went sailing. Then he saw the temple wall pass under him. The top of the pillar was carrying him out over the cliff, over the sheer drop to the sea far below!

THUD! The middle of the pillar hit the temple wall and Dr. Cooper was knocked free by the impact, tumbling headlong toward the ocean.

OOF! The harness he was still wearing came to the end of its rope, and he snapped to an abrupt halt in midair, dangling from the pillar like a puppet on a string.

The base of the pillar began to rise. Bill, Jeff, and Jay grabbed the ropes dangling from it, hoping to hold it down and keep the pillar from flipping over the wall entirely. All three were lifted off their feet, but they hung on anyway, hoping, praying.

Up went their end of the pillar, higher, higher, as Dr. Cooper's end lowered him toward the sea.

Then, with not a man, not a pound, not a single ounce to spare, the pillar came to rest on the temple wall with each end suspended in air, perfectly but precariously balanced: Dr. Cooper dangling from one end, Bill, Jeff, and Jay dangling from the other.

"Oh man," Bill drawled, "now what?"

"Hang on," Lila screamed. "Just hang on!"

There was a low, grating noise. The pillar was beginning to roll along the wall like a big rolling pin, reeling in the ropes from which Jay, Bill, and Jeff were hanging, along with the harness that still held Dr. Cooper.

Dr. Cooper looked below and saw nothing but ocean waves and a tiny, distant barge; he looked above and saw the face of Zeus coming around, then coming around again, much closer, as the pillar kept rotating and reeling him in.

As Lila stepped hurriedly along the wall, approaching the pillar even as it rumbled and rolled slowly toward her, she looked for a stone, a stick, anything large enough to jam under the pillar to wedge it to a stop.

Dr. Cooper ran out of rope. "AWWW!" He was

hauled over the top of the pillar as it turned, held fast by the harness around his body and feeling like a roast pig on a spit. If only he had a knife!

Then Bill's rope ran out and the rough surface of the pillar broke his grip. With a cry of pain, he fell to the temple floor.

Out of balance! The base of the pillar began to rise, the top began to sink.

Lila hopped onto the pillar, step-step-stepping as it rotated under her feet, inching her way out from the wall and toward the base where Jay and Jeff were getting tangled in the ropes. No good. She wasn't even half Bill's weight. The pillar was still rolling and tilting toward the sea.

CHUNK! Somebody jammed a stone under the pillar, and it stopped rolling. A man leaped from the wall to the lower end of the pillar, and it sank under his weight.

Back in balance!

"Lila!" Dr. Cooper hollered. "Bring your knife!"

The stranger, a man with blond hair, nodded to her. "Go ahead. I think we can keep it in balance now."

She stepped carefully along the pillar, balancing herself, until she reached the wall. She could see her father, one hand clinging to Zeus's eye and his foot planted in Zeus's mouth, struggling to free himself from the harness. She looked back. The stranger was helping Jay and Jeff untangle themselves.

She stepped out on the pillar, nothing but a sheer drop to the ocean below her, and inched her way out toward her father, the knife in her trembling hand.

The stranger had his own knife and cut away the ropes that had tangled around Jay and Jeff. With his help, they climbed on top of the pillar and sat on it.

"Just like a teeter-totter," said Jay.

But Lila was still edging toward the other end, toward her father.

"Uh . . ." Jay asked the stranger, "how much do you weigh?"

"About one-sixty," the man replied.

Jay looked down at Bill, who was still dusting himself off after his fall. "Bill? How much do you weigh?"

"Two thirty," Bill replied.

The stranger asked Jay, "How much does your sister weigh?"

"Enough," was all Jay answered as their end of the pillar began to rise.

Dr. Cooper took the knife from Lila's hand as he felt the pillar pitch down toward the ocean again. "Lila! Get back! Get off the pillar!"

She spun around and tried to run back. The pillar pitched some more and she slipped. Her fingers dug into hieroglyphics and her foot came to rest on Zeus's beard as the pillar sagged and rocked and the stones in the wall started crumbling.

Jay, Jeff, and the stranger moved as far back as they could, but the pillar was beginning to slide through the wall and there was no stopping it.

"It's gonna go!" Jeff hollered.

Dr. Cooper sliced through the harness rope and got free. "Go, Lila, *go!*"

She crawled, scrambled, and made it to the wall. Now the pillar was sliding past her, bucking and scraping over the stones.

Dr. Cooper grabbed at Zeus's beard, then some hieroglyphics, then some relief carvings, climbing up the downsliding pillar and getting nowhere until he ran out of pillar to climb on. A hand reached out to grab his just as the pillar slid free of the wall and plummeted toward the seashore below. In an instant, Jay, Jeff, and the stranger yanked him to safety atop the wall.

The pillar dropped silently, as if in slow motion, growing smaller and smaller, until it dove into the sandy beach like a spear, making the ground quiver—and making Dr. Cooper wince.

It teetered there a moment then tipped like a big tree toward the ocean . . . directly toward the waiting barge as the barge crew dove for the water.

KAWHUMP! The barge bucked, rolled, and almost capsized from the impact. A mighty wave washed up on the shore.

Lila shut her eyes. They all held their breath. They could hear the last mist from the huge splash hiss down upon the surface of the water.

And then . . . it was quiet.

"Well whaddaya know . . ." Bill muttered.

Lila ventured a peek and saw the barge rocking a little but still afloat. The pillar, with Zeus glaring up at them, was lying in the barge a little crooked and with one end hanging out, but none the worse for wear. The barge crew paddled around in the water, wide-eyed and upset, but safe.

Dr. Cooper started breathing again. His kids, his crewmen, and the stranger could only sit there on the wall, shaken, dusty, thankful to be alive, and totally amazed.

At last Dr. Cooper found his voice and said, "Well . . . we got it on the barge."

Silence. Somber faces.

And then Bill cracked a smile. Jeff snorted a laugh through his nose. Jay burst right out laughing. Dr. Cooper allowed himself a smile, then a grin, then a laugh, shaking his head in amazement. When Lila saw her father laughing, she figured everything was okay and began to laugh too. They all started hugging and shaking hands, happy to be alive, happy with success.

"I don't believe it!" said Lila.

"God works in wondrous ways," said Dr. Cooper.

"Boy, doesn't He!" replied the stranger, shaking Jacob Cooper's hand.

Then, looking at the man directly for the first time, Dr. Cooper recognized him. "Brent! Brent Anderson!"

Brent Anderson smiled broadly. "Hi, Jake. Working?"

"Can't you tell?"

They both laughed and then embraced like old buddies.

"What in the world are you doing here?" Dr. Cooper asked.

"I came to find you."

"Jay! Lila! Meet an old friend of mine, Brent Anderson! He's a missionary to Africa."

"Was," said Brent, shaking hands with Jay and Lila. "And, hopefully, will be again."

Dr. Cooper could hear trouble in Brent's voice. "What's happened?"

Brent's face became grim. "Idi Nkromo and his revolution. He and his military have taken over most of the country of Togwana."

Dr. Cooper nodded with recollection. "He's been in the news lately. A rather dangerous character, I understand."

"Oh, he likes killing anyone who stands in his way, or questions his actions, or doubts his power—and mostly, he hates Christians. He's ordered the churches closed; he's killed and imprisoned believers. Sandy and I barely got out of the country alive."

Bill and Jeff could sense a serious conversation coming. "Uh, Jake, we'll start stowing the gear," said Bill.

"Thanks, guys," Dr. Cooper replied.

The two men made their way back along the wall. Jay and Lila got up and were about to leave them alone, too, but their father said quietly, "Stick around." They sat back down on the wall beside their father.

Dr. Cooper's voice was quiet and compassionate. "You got out all right? You and Sandy and the kids?"

"Yes, we're fine. They're back in the States now. I'm on staff with the mission board until . . ." Brent smiled wistfully.

Jacob Cooper knew his friend. "You're thinking of going back to Togwana?"

Brent nodded. "I'm not finished there, Jake. There's one last tribe of people who live across the desert who have never heard the gospel. Rumor has it they're a deadly bunch, headhunters and cannibals who would just as soon eat strangers as welcome them. But God wants me to take the gospel to those people, and I believe I will, Idi Nkromo or no Idi Nkromo. It'll happen, Jake."

Dr. Cooper admired faith like that. "I'm sure it will."

Now Brent looked his friend in the eye. "Good, because you just might be a part of it."

Jacob Cooper raised one eyebrow and then exchanged a glance with his kids. "Is this going to be dangerous?"

Brent nodded. "It might be."

"Count us in," said Jay, which brought him a corrective look from Lila.

Dr. Cooper wanted to hear more. "How can we help?"

Brent Anderson looked over his shoulder, and they all followed his glance across the excavation. There, looking almost ghostly in long, wraparound garments and intricate, bone jewelry, stood two Africans, apparently men of high office in their country. They were both tall and powerful, with eyes that could bore holes right through you.

"Strange things are happening in Togwana, Jake, things that no one can explain, and that's why I'm here. These men were sent by the Chief Secretary of the Republic of Togwana." Brent gave Dr. Cooper a probing look. "They came to find a

13

spiritual man, a man close to God with wisdom to solve great mysteries. They first came to me in America, but I've brought them to you."

As Jacob Cooper looked into the burning eyes of the two towering visitors, he had a feeling he and his kids would soon be going to Africa.

TWO

When their plane finally landed in Togwana, the Coopers saw military jeeps and trucks parked near the tiny airport terminal. Soldiers were standing about in khaki uniforms and black berets, and even two weather-beaten Russian MIGs were parked under some palm trees. Obviously, a military government was in charge now—in charge of *everything*.

As she looked out the airplane window, Lila couldn't help wondering aloud, "What are we walking into?"

"A brave new world under Togwana's new dictator," answered an attractive African-American woman in her late thirties sitting in the seat directly behind them. She immediately extended her hand. "Dr. Jennifer Henderson, Stanford University."

Dr. Cooper gripped her hand. "Uh . . . Jacob Cooper, and this is my son, Jay, and my daughter, Lila."

"I suppose you were invited by Bernard and Walter back there?"

The Coopers shot a discreet glance toward the

rear of the plane where the two somber gentlemen from Togwana were sitting. They'd given their names as Bernard and Walter.

"They wanted somebody who knows rocks," Dr. Henderson explained, "and that's why they invited me. I'm a geologist. How about you?"

"I'm an archaeologist," Dr. Cooper answered. He could have mentioned that he was founder of the Cooper Institute for Biblical Archaeology and specialized in ancient civilizations of the Bible, but he said no more than necessary. The Coopers couldn't be sure who this woman really was; they didn't know if she could be trusted.

"So they want at least two professional opinions regarding their little mystery," said Dr. Henderson.

"I'll be interested to know just what the mystery is," said Dr. Cooper. "The letter from the Chief Secretary was rather vague."

"The Chief Secretary is supposed to be meeting us with a car—and some more information, I hope."

Bernard and Walter helped carry their luggage and led them to a gate that passed through the airport security fence. It was there that they met a quick-stepping, uniformed man with braids on his shoulder and medals on his chest. He smiled broadly and beckoned to them with fluttery little waves from both hands. "Hello! Doctors Henderson and Cooper, yes?" He offered his hand in greeting. "D. M. Mobutu, Chief Secretary of the Republic of Togwana!"

Dr. Cooper shook his hand. "Dr. Jacob Cooper, at your service. These are my children, Jay and Lila."

He shook their hands vigorously, almost comically.

Then he came to Dr. Henderson and had a special greeting for her. "Ahhh, Dr. Henderson, I have looked forward to this moment." With a graceful flourish, he took her hand and kissed it.

She stuck to business. "And I've looked forward to the challenge of the work we're here to do. How soon can we get started?"

Mobutu surveyed the sky. "The weather is improving. You may get your first glimpse of our little problem on the way to the presidential palace."

Dr. Cooper was puzzled. "I'd like that. We're all eager to hear the details of your situation—"

"Come! We have a car waiting!" He called to the two escorts, "Philip! Thomas! Bring their bags!"

"Don't you mean Bernard and Walter?" Dr. Cooper hinted.

"Oh, yes," Mobutu quickly agreed, "Bernard and Walter. Yes!"

Instead of going through the small terminal, they hurried down a narrow walk under a thick canopy of trees and out to a side street. Waiting there was a long, white limousine with tinted windows. Bernard and Walter loaded the luggage into the trunk while Mobutu opened the big passenger door.

"Air conditioned," he said proudly.

The American guests were ready for that and got inside. Bernard and Walter, their mission completed, hurried up a trail into the jungle and were gone.

When the driver hit the accelerator and the limousine lurched away from the curb, it felt like a getaway.

Mobutu sat with them, trying to maintain his cordial smile but looking nervous. He peered out the windows as the limousine raced along the narrow road, first through green jungle then past crude farms and small, mud homesteads.

Dr. Cooper tried to get a conversation going. "So . . . you work for President Nkromo, is that correct?"

Mobutu smiled broadly. "Oh, yes. As chief secretary, I am quite close to the president. I am his special assistant." Then he added with emphasis, "And our new government is working very well. The president is powerful. He has brought order to our country!"

Dr. Cooper simply nodded and smiled. He could sense that Mobutu was having trouble believing his own glowing boasts.

The limousine entered the ragged, unimproved outskirts of Nkromotown, still mostly small homes, barns, and chicken coops made from mud brick, and occasionally, concrete. People and pigs, children and chickens, cattle and oxen wandered freely in the fields, thickets, and side streets.

"You should know," Mobutu suddenly blurted, "that bringing you to Togwana was not the president's idea."

Instantly, all their eyes were upon him.

Mobutu continued, visibly nervous. "I must tell you, the president has little use for outsiders, and

18

even less use for advice, even from those close to him. He does not wish to appear weak or in need of help from anyone."

Dr. Cooper exchanged a glance with the others and then asked, "Is this the reason for the secrecy? Avoiding the airport terminal, racing away in this car, and calling your two men Bernard and Walter?"

Mobutu nodded. "Bernard and Walter do not wish their real names attached to this enterprise in case it should . . ." he had to wrestle the words out of his throat, "in case it should fail."

Dr. Cooper's voice was firm. "Mr. Mobutu, is the president even aware that we're here?"

"Oh, yes," Mobutu replied with an emphatic nod. "Yes, he knows you're here, and he does not disapprove. It's just that . . . " Mobutu's eyes dropped, "he consented grudgingly and warned me that no one should know about it." Then he leaned forward and spoke in a lowered voice, "But you should know, I offered to bring in a geologist and an archaeologist. I did not tell him I would bring in someone with . . . uh . . . *spiritual* credentials as well."

Dr. Cooper began to ask, "Are you referring to the fact that I and my children are—"

"Shh!" Mobutu held up his hand. "Do not speak it. Do not even think it while you are in this country. President Nkromo has already banished thousands who are of your . . . religious persuasion. Those who did not leave were arrested, put into forced labor, and some . . . were executed."

Jacob Cooper's voice had a sharp edge as he

asked, "And yet you brought us here anyway, knowing it could endanger our lives?"

Mobutu bowed a little, acting humble. "Dr. Cooper, this problem we have will take more than a mere scientist to solve."

Jennifer Henderson raised an eyebrow at that remark, but Mobutu continued, "It could require someone with eyes to see *beyond* what is visible."

Dr. Cooper's eyes narrowed as he replied, "Mr. Mobutu, you have much to explain."

But instead of explaining, Mobutu leaned close to the window, looked at the weather, and then rapped on the glass panel that separated them from the driver. The driver looked back, Mobutu shouted some instructions, and almost immediately the driver took a hard left turn off the main road, up a steep, winding road into the hills.

"We're not going into the city?" Dr. Cooper asked.

"No," Mobutu replied, "not yet."

"Where are you taking us?"

"You need to see the Stone first," Mobutu answered, "and then we will talk further."

"The . . . Stone?"

Mobutu added quietly, "We call it a *baloa-kota,* which means an omen, an evil sign. It is why we brought you here. Many, including the president, believe the Stone is magic."

Dr. Henderson was dismayed. "You brought us all the way to Africa just to look at a *rock?*"

Mobutu only smiled at her. "This is your profession, yes?"

A few minutes later, the limousine reached the top of a hill, swerved off the road into some gravel, and lurched to a halt. Then the driver, in his neatly pressed uniform and his cap squarely in place on his head, got out, walked back, and swung the door open with a flourish.

Mobutu stepped out and waited courteously by the door. "Please," he beckoned.

Dr. Cooper, still unsure of the group's safety, ventured a look outside, then stepped out. "It's all right."

The others followed.

They had parked on a lofty bluff overlooking the city and the rolling, jungled hills stretching to the east. The clouds were dissolving away in the afternoon sun and the view was wide, sweeping, and beautiful. Nkromotown was a small city of white stone, gray concrete, and red tile. Dr. Cooper could see a cluster of large stone buildings in the center of the city, most likely the presidential palace and parliament hall now occupied by Nkromo and his military leaders.

"A beautiful city, Mr. Mobutu," he said, turning to look at the Chief Secretary, then turning some more, trying to find him. "A beautiful country, and—"

The sentence died on his lips as he looked toward the west across the vast, rugged drylands. Mobutu was standing on the edge of the bluff with Jennifer Henderson, Jay, and Lila, looking toward the west and then back at him, obviously wanting to see his reaction.

Dr. Cooper didn't know how to react. He didn't

even know what to believe. He blinked, then rubbed his eyes. *I can't be seeing what I think I'm seeing*, he thought.

"Dad . . ." said Jay, his voice a hushed whisper. Apparently he was seeing it too.

"What . . . is that?" Lila asked. "How does it—"

"Is this a mirage?" asked Dr. Henderson.

Mobutu shook his head. "No mirage, Dr. Henderson. What you are seeing is really there."

The clouds continued to thin out, unveiling . . . a wall? A sheer cliff? A towering plateau?

Whatever it was, it totally filled the gap between two mountain cliffs to the north and south, and stretched from the desert floor to a height above the clouds.

"How far away is it?" asked Dr. Cooper, certain his eyes were being deceived.

Mobutu estimated, "From this point, about eighteen kilometers."

"Ten miles!" Dr. Henderson exclaimed.

"Then it's as big as it looks," concluded Dr. Cooper.

"It's a *mountain!*" Lila said, her voice hushed with awe.

The sun was moving toward the west now, so the surface details were in shade and hard to discern. But the shape was stark against the sky, obscured in only a few places by high, fluffy clouds: a rectangle of stone, a huge block, square at the corners, sheer and vertical at either end, and, as far as they could tell, perfectly flat on top. And Lila was right: it was nothing less than a mountain.

"How . . ." Dr. Cooper had trouble finding his breath. "How tall is it?"

"Nearly four kilometers, as close as we can tell."

"That's over ten thousand feet!" Jay exclaimed.

"And we figure it's at least eight kilometers long and two kilometers wide," Mobutu added.

"How long has it been here?" Dr. Cooper asked.

"Just a few weeks, doctor," Mobutu answered. "From here we used to be able to see past those mountain cliffs and cross the flat desert. Now the entire western half of Togwana is hidden from view."

Dr. Henderson actually sank to the ground, overcome by the sight. "Stone? It's of stone?"

"We think it is."

"But how did it get there? What caused it?"

Mobutu frowned. "Dr. Henderson, we hired *you* to answer such questions."

She only shook her head. "But this is . . . this is impossible. Nothing of this size and shape has ever occurred before in nature!"

"And so we call it a *baloa-kota*," Mobutu said somberly. "A dreaded curse, a plague sent upon us! And now you see it with your own eyes: the Stone of Togwana!"

In the presidential palace, a young butler in a green tuxedo swung open the huge, mahogany doors and announced, "Your Excellency, the Chief Secretary with his honored guests!"

They entered the presidential chamber, a room that resembled a cathedral with a high, arched ceiling, stained-glass windows, and pillared, marble walls. At the far end of the room, at the end of a long avenue of red carpet, His Excellency, President and Field Marshal Idi Nkromo, sat behind a desk the size of a battleship. The medals on his chest glittering like a Christmas tree, Nkromo glowered at them, his eyes big and bulging with anger. On the exquisitely paneled wall behind him, a ten-foot high portrait of himself glared with the same angry expression, only twice as big.

"I am Oz, the great and powerful!" Jay whispered, and Lila gave him a corrective poke.

They marched forward, Mobutu at the head, then stood shoulder-to-shoulder in a straight line before His Excellency.

"Your Excellency," Mobutu announced, his spine straight as a rod, "I present to you the scientists from America: Dr. Jennifer Henderson, geologist; and Dr. Jacob Cooper, archaeologist!"

Nkromo gestured toward Jay and Lila, his eyes sending the question to Mobutu. "And . . . ?"

Mobutu blurted, "And Dr. Cooper's two children, Jay and Lila."

Nkromo looked at Dr. Henderson, then Dr. Cooper, then Jay and Lila, his face betraying not the slightest hint of favor at their presence. Then, at long last, he spoke, his voice deep, loud, and intimidating. "I welcome you to the Republic of Togwana! We will do well for each other, yes? You will remove the Stone, and I will pay you well."

"Yes," Dr. Henderson ventured, "we do need to discuss our fee before we—"

"How long will it take?" Nkromo interrupted.

They had no answer; they weren't sure they had even grasped the question.

Dr. Cooper gave a slight bow and said, "Your Excellency, we have only just arrived and know very little about the Stone. If it pleases you, we need to venture into the desert and study it closely to learn what it is and where it came from."

"And how to make it go away, yes?"

Dr. Henderson picked it up from there. "We'll need vehicles and equipment, food and water—"

Nkromo waved her off and declared, "Mr. Mobutu will see to that. Whatever you need, he will supply it."

"Thank you, sir," said Dr. Cooper.

Nkromo rose from his chair; Mobutu took one step backward and the four guests did the same. Then the president patted his big belly and admired the towering portrait of himself. "If I want something done, it will be done, you see? I had ten witch doctors, but they could not make the Stone go away. They could not move it. They could not even make it smaller." He shook his head with regret. "So I ordered their heads smashed in with stones."

Lila gasped. She didn't mean to, it just happened.

His Excellency was pleased at that response. "So, you will not fail, I know. You are scientists from America! You know about rocks! You will please me, I know."

Dr. Cooper tried to keep his voice even as he asked, "Are we to understand, sir, that you expect us to *remove* the Stone?"

25

"Yes! Take it away!" Nkromo bellowed with an angry wave of his arm. "Remove it far from here, I don't care where! It must not remain in the path of His Excellency!" Then he raised his hands toward them as if to grant a blessing, but the tone of his voice sounded more like a threat. "May you have success!"

THREE

As they hurried across the palace grounds, intent on getting out of there, Dr. Henderson was the first to speak. "Well, I've heard enough. I'm getting on the first plane out of here!"

"If you try to leave Togwana without permission, you will be shot," Mobutu said flatly.

Dr. Henderson's mouth dropped open. "You can't be serious!"

"You're forgetting, this is an African dictatorship," said Dr. Cooper. "Nkromo can do whatever he wants."

"Nkromo is out of his mind!" said Dr. Henderson.

Mobutu cautioned her with frantic little waves of his hand. "No! Never speak ill of the president!" He lowered his voice to share some inside advice. "Even if he is crazy, that doesn't matter! What matters is that he gets what he wants or people die—even you."

"But this is an incredible freak of nature, so huge it's mind-boggling! If Nkromo couldn't move it with all his army, what are *we* supposed to do?"

"But we don't even know what it is yet!" Jay countered.

"And I'm dying to find out," said Lila.

"Well, I don't care to die at all!" Jennifer Henderson snapped.

"Dr. Henderson," said Dr. Cooper softly, touching her shoulder to comfort her, "we could be staring an incredible discovery right in the face, and we'd be untrue to our professions if we ran from it. As for Nkromo, it's obvious he's afraid of it. It's something he doesn't understand and can't control. If we can give him some answers, his attitude might change."

Dr. Henderson finally calmed down a bit and nodded. "Well . . . what other choice do we have anyway?"

Dr. Cooper looked at Lila as he addressed Mobutu. "We have a list for you." Lila pulled several sheets of paper from her pocket and handed them to Mobutu as her father continued, "We'll need vehicles, surveying equipment . . ."

"Seismic equipment," Dr. Henderson added, "and a core drill."

"Oh, and I'll need an airplane, single engine, high wing, with short take-off and landing capability." Dr. Cooper waved at the list. "It's all on there."

Mobutu scanned the long list with widening eyes.

"Oh," said Lila, pulling out another sheet of paper. "And here's a grocery list."

"Come on," said Dr. Cooper. "Let's have a look at that thing."

After a meal and a change into cooler clothes, the Coopers and Dr. Henderson were ready for their

28

first trek into the rugged drylands of western Togwana. They were riding in a land rover provided by Mr. Mobutu—it was the first item on the list. Mr. Mobutu came along, not because he wanted to but because Nkromo required it.

The road into the desert was unimproved but apparently well-traveled, at least by Nkromo's armies. It meandered for mile after mile across a dead, forbidding landscape of wind-carved stone pinnacles and deep, eroded gullies, of sun-baked, jagged rocks and blowing sand. With each mile they drove, the Stone grew larger and its top edge higher and more directly overhead, until finally they entered the Stone's afternoon shadow—miles and miles of shadow, as if the sun had disappeared behind a perfectly straight-edged bank of clouds. Jay and Lila had to stick their heads out the windows to see the Stone's top edge thousands of feet above them, black against the flare of the hidden sun.

Dr. Cooper brought the rover to a halt, and they stepped out onto the barren landscape to have a look.

Jay scanned the Stone's top edge with some binoculars, the magnified image quivering from the excitement coursing through him. "I think I see some ice up there. Guess that puts the summit above the freezing level."

"Any features of any kind?" Dr. Cooper asked.

"Nope. That top edge is so straight it looks the same with or without binoculars."

Jacob Cooper shook his head in awe. "Any thoughts, Dr. Henderson?"

Jennifer Henderson seemed transfixed as she stared at the stone.

"Dr. Henderson?" Dr. Cooper asked again, a little concerned.

She looked at him startled, as if awakened from a spell. "What? Oh. No, Dr. Cooper. It reminds me of basaltic columns such as Devil's Tower in Wyoming, . . . but this is nothing like that. I don't see how this can be a natural occurrence." She allowed some of her fear to show as she added, "And I'm not sure we should approach any closer."

Dr. Cooper respected her concerns. "Lila, get out the Geiger counter. We'd better check for radiation." There was no response. "Lila?"

Lila was standing by herself a short distance away, motionless, gazing upon the Stone as if seeing a vision.

Her dad approached her quietly. "Lila? What is it?"

She heard his question and looked his way, but could not think of an answer—at least, nothing that would sound scientific. Scientific observation was done with the eyes, with the ears, with tools and instruments; she was *feeling* something with her heart, something she had no words to describe. Great symphonies made her feel this way. Beautiful sunsets. A Bible verse spoken or read at just the right time.

"I don't know, Dad," she said at last, her voice hushed. "It's just . . . it's just wonderful, that's all."

Dr. Henderson disagreed. "I think it could be dangerous!"

"I'm not afraid," she countered. "I want to get closer. I want to touch it."

"Same here," said Jay, bringing the Geiger counter. He turned it on and twisted the dials. "No radiation. I guess it's safe."

"If it is a *boloa-kota*," Mobutu said, "it can never be safe!"

"Well . . ." Dr. Cooper stared up at the Stone, scratching his head. "While we're this far away, why don't we take some readings with the transit and get some dimensions?"

They worked as a team, pacing, measuring, peering through an engineer's transit and calculating. By late afternoon, they had some numbers.

"The side facing us runs roughly north and south," Jay said, reviewing his notes. "We don't know about the other sides yet because we can't see them from here, but anyway . . ." He scribbled, then erased, then scribbled again. "If I didn't make any mistakes, the side facing us is right around 20,380 feet long and 9,348 high. That's, uh . . ." he tapped out the figures on his pocket calculator, ". . . 3.86 miles long and 1.77 miles high."

He handed his notes across the hood of the land rover to his father. Dr. Cooper whistled his amazement as Dr. Henderson came alongside to study Jay's scribblings. She could only shake her head as she read them.

"Well done, Jay," said Dr. Cooper. "Now we're ready for the next step."

"Which is?" Dr. Henderson asked.

"We've found out all we can from a distance. Now we're going to have to walk right up and touch it."

"We could be waking a sleeping lion," Mobutu cautioned.

31

"I don't disagree. But I would find it more unbearable to remain here, not knowing, not learning. We still have about three hours of daylight."

Dr. Henderson shifted her gaze toward the Stone, its surface flat, smooth, and unblemished, its color a dull, volcanic red. She didn't bother to disguise her dread even as she agreed. "So let's go touch it—but keep the motor running."

The Stone looked like a monstrous wall directly in front of them and continued to loom larger and larger as they approached. After they had driven five kilometers, the south end was fully to their left, the north end was fully to their right, and the top edge was almost straight above them. It made them dizzy to look up at it.

"Perfectly vertical!" Dr. Henderson exclaimed. "Perfectly flat!"

"Hey," said Jay, "I think I see the base!"

They had just come over a small rise. Dr. Cooper eased the rover to a halt. A half mile ahead, they could see the desert road coming to an abrupt end where the Stone now lay across it. But it wasn't just the road that ended here. The whole desert—sand, stones, brush, rock formations, *everything*—ended here as well. Abruptly, cleanly as if cut with a knife, the desert was now divided by a laser-straight wall of reddish stone that seemed limitless as it stretched north and south and soared into the sky.

Dr. Cooper looked north through the binoculars, then south. "The Stone is butting up against sheer cliffs at either end. I don't know if we'll be able to drive around it. It may even be impossible to hike around."

"The Stone is in the path of His Excellency!" Jay quipped, recalling Nkromo's angry words. "Makes me wonder what's on the other side."

"Nooo," Mobutu cautioned with a wag of his head. "You don't want to go over there. It's the land of the Motosas, a desert tribe of cannibals and headhunters. They are ruthless and bloodthirsty, a real problem we've been trying to eliminate."

Dr. Cooper considered that a moment. "Well, it seems you now have a wall to keep them contained."

Mobutu only scowled and said nothing further.

"Shall we proceed?" Dr. Cooper asked.

"Hard hats, everyone," Dr. Henderson cautioned. "If any debris or ice breaks loose, it'll fall straight down on top of us."

They grabbed their yellow hard hats and put them on. Then Dr. Cooper put the rover in gear and let it tiptoe steadily forward, the idle of the engine and the quiet crunching of its tires over the sand and rock the only sounds. Finally, about fifty feet from the face of the Stone, he braked to a stop and turned off the engine.

Now there was a silence so absolute they could hear the blood rushing through their ears, the *tick, tick* of the cooling engine, and the little creaks and groans of the rover anytime somebody moved.

They looked at Dr. Henderson. This was her moment.

She stepped out of the rover and walked carefully,

almost tiptoeing, toward the vast, reddish wall in front of her. The others followed: Jacob Cooper just a few steps behind, Jay and Lila a few steps behind him, and Mobutu a considerable distance back. Dr. Henderson paused several times to look straight up, but kept putting one foot in front of the other until cautiously, furtively, with outstretched hand, she touched the face of the Stone.

Nothing happened. The "sleeping lion" kept sleeping, at least for the moment.

As the others watched, eager to hear her verdict, Dr. Henderson brushed her fingers lightly over the surface, then studied it carefully, scanning back and forth, up and down. They could see she was getting agitated. Reaching into her tool belt, she took out a magnifying glass and studied the Stone's surface very closely, her nose only an inch away.

When she finally turned to look back at them, her face was filled with wonder and fear. "It appears to be *man-made!*"

Man-made? They stood there gawking at the Stone, waiting for belief to set in.

"Oooohh . . ." With a timid, trembling cry, shaking his head in fear and denial, Mobutu backed away.

"All *right!*" Jay blurted, clenching his fist happily. A rock this size was intriguing, of course, but a *man-made* rock this size meant a real mystery!

Dr. Cooper hurried forward and touched the Stone himself.

"You see it?" Dr. Henderson asked him excitedly. "See the tool marks? Someone cut this thing out.

They *carved* it. This isn't a natural occurrence at all!"

Jacob Cooper could see what Dr. Henderson was talking about. Though the marks were very fine and indiscernible from a distance, the surface did betray some kind of highly skilled handwork. He stepped back several paces and looked straight up the immense wall. "That could explain the symmetry, the unnatural, square shape, the straight lines and ninety-degree corners." He returned to touch the Stone's surface again and study it closely. "Ancient stonework . . ." he muttered. "Stonecutting that would have made Solomon proud." He looked straight up the wall, his chin almost resting against it. "This thing was *designed*. But it would have taken years, even centuries to complete! Mr. Mobutu!"

Mobutu answered from a safe distance. "Yes, Dr. Cooper?"

"Tell me again how the stone appeared. You say it's been here a few weeks and no one knows how it came to be here?"

"That's right, doctor. When we all went to bed, the desert was the same as it has been for centuries. When we got up the next morning, this object was here, just as you see it today."

Jacob Cooper slowly wagged his head, at a total loss. "Who could cut out such a huge stone and place it in this desert overnight?"

"And what did they cut it out of?" Dr. Henderson asked. "Imagine the size of the quarry, or the hole that must be left after the stone was removed . . ."

"Maybe it's a meteor," Jay suggested, touching it. "It just fell here from outer space."

"The most gentle meteor in history to touch down so lightly," his dad replied. "No crater, no fire, no signs of an impact."

Lila came close and rested her palms against the smooth surface. *Yes,* she thought. *There's that feeling again. It's like a grand symphony, like a loving embrace, or a warm fire on a cold night.*

Jay was still theorizing. "Maybe some ancient civilization figured out a way to make this thing materialize here from another dimension."

Dr. Cooper built on that idea. "So maybe it's an illusion, a kind of holographic phenomenon . . ."

Lila pressed her ear against the red surface as if listening for sounds. Like finding a familiar face in a crowd, like finding your way again after being lost— that's how the Stone made her feel.

Dr. Henderson became sarcastic. "Or maybe it was planted here by extraterrestrials. Come *on.*"

Dr. Cooper had to laugh, if only to relieve his frustration. "I think we'd better gather some more data before we go any further with theories!"

"Maybe *God* put it here!" said Lila, her face still against the Stone.

Jennifer Henderson only sniffed at that, but Dr. Cooper and Jay paused and looked at her.

"What makes you say that, Lila?" her dad asked.

She hesitated to answer, then finally said, "It just *feels* like God put it here."

"Well," Dr. Henderson laughed, "that's as good an explanation as any I've heard so far!"

Lila broke away from the Stone's surface and glared at her. "Who else do you know who can create something out of nothing, overnight?"

Dr. Henderson was ready to argue. "Young lady, this object was not created out of nothing! It's basalt and silica, the very rock and sand you're standing on! Here, just look." She removed a small pick from her belt and struck the surface to break off a sample.

The steel tool bounced off with a metallic ring but didn't leave a mark. Indignant, Dr. Henderson struck the surface again, but with the same result.

"Basalt?" Dr. Cooper asked with one eyebrow raised.

"We'll wait for that core drill," Dr. Henderson answered, unruffled, putting the pick back in her belt.

Jay was intrigued and touched the Stone, holding his hand against it. "What if God *did* put it here?"

Dr. Henderson lowered her voice, but she was angry. "Well, that would make a nice tale for the Togwanans, wouldn't it? They're superstitious. They resort to religion and spiritualism to explain things they don't understand. Let's just tell them God put it here, and we can all go home a little sooner!"

Dr. Cooper tried to calm her. "Dr. Henderson, belief in God doesn't rule out scientific method and research. No one's saying that."

"But scientific research doesn't rule out God either," Lila added.

Then Mobutu jumped in, and he was angry. "People, you were not hired to discuss religion! You were hired to explain why this stone is here and to find a way to remove it!"

"We have to consider all theories," Dr. Cooper informed him.

"So let's get on with the *scientific* research," said Dr. Henderson, really dwelling on the word *scientific* to rub it in.

"Well, okay." Jay was ready with another possibility. "If this thing really is man-made, then it has to serve some purpose. I'll bet there are rooms and passages inside, maybe burial chambers like in the pyramids. If we can get inside those rooms, that would tell us something."

"The seismic equipment will tell us if there are any cavities inside," said Dr. Cooper.

Dr. Henderson sighed in frustration. "In order to use it, we'll have to get on top."

They all looked at the vertical, featureless, red wall before them. Climbing was out of the question.

"Mr. Mobutu," said Dr. Cooper, "what's the latest on that airplane?"

FOUR

At Nkromo International Airport the next day, Mobutu introduced the Coopers and Dr. Henderson to a single-engine, high-winged Cessna, apparently one of Idi Nkromo's private fleet of aircraft. It was big enough to haul four people and a limited amount of gear. Mr. Mobutu, already afraid of the Stone, was even more afraid of flying, so he kindly offered to stay behind.

Jay and Lila climbed into the backseat and fastened their seat belts. Dr. Cooper took the pilot's seat up front, and Dr. Henderson sat in the seat to his right.

Mobutu came up to the pilot's window and stuck his hand through. "May God grant you a safe journey," he said quietly.

Dr. Cooper smiled, gripping Mobutu's hand. "See you soon."

Within minutes, they were flying over the desert and toward the Stone. From the air it was as big as a mountain, and still higher than they were.

Dr. Cooper was watching the altimeter. "All right, Jay, now we'll find out how close your calculations were. We're climbing through five thousand right now. If you're right, another five or six thousand should put us over the top of that thing."

Soon the Stone filled their vision, rising above the flat desert like an out-of-place, rectangular skyscraper. Dr. Cooper made a slow left turn so they could circle around the south end. The airplane had climbed to nine thousand feet, and they were still below the Stone's summit.

"Take a look at that," said Dr. Cooper, pointing below. "Rugged cliffs at either end of the Stone make it almost impossible to travel around, and the only road through the desert goes right under it! Half of Nkromo's country is on the other side!"

"Beyond his reach," said Dr. Henderson.

"Exactly. If he can't reach that part of the country he can't control the people who live there. No wonder he's so upset!"

The plane continued climbing as it headed south. At nine thousand and eight hundred feet, everyone looked out the right side. Since the desert floor was about 1,500 feet above sea level, they had to be within a thousand feet of the Stone's estimated altitude; soon they would see the top.

Ten thousand feet. The Stone still looked perfectly flat. Then the plane rounded the far southern corner and for the first time they could see another side.

"Incredible!" Dr. Henderson exclaimed.

Jay and Lila were both leaning close to the window on the right, staring in wonder at the Stone's south-facing surface. It too was perfectly flat, perfectly smooth. It met the eastern surface at a precise, ninety-degree angle.

"It's shaped just like a big box!" Jay exclaimed, snapping some pictures.

Ten thousand, nine hundred. They could see the top.

"This is impossible!" said Dr. Henderson. "There is no way in the world!"

"It's not a box," said Lila. "It's a huge block!"

It was all Dr. Cooper could do to keep his mind on flying the plane and his eyes on the instruments. He continued to climb to eleven thousand feet. Below them now, sitting solidly on the desert floor like a brick on a table, was an immense, mountain-sized object that was rectangular in shape: two long sides, two narrow sides, and a flat top, the same color on every side.

They continued circling around to the west side. The western surface looked identical to the eastern, the same smooth, featureless red stone.

"Okay," said Dr. Henderson, looking through binoculars. "I see the desert road coming out the other side."

They all looked, and Jay snapped more pictures. There it was, all right, winding along, crossing more desert, then grassy drylands, and finally disappearing into some rugged, wooded hills in the west.

Lila peered through her binoculars and spotted something. "Hey, I think I see a village down there!"

"Where?" Dr. Henderson asked, training her binoculars downward.

"Uh . . . about a mile off the northwest corner, on

the other side of the grassland, where that forest begins."

"Got it. Oh, it's a big one. At least . . . sixty structures."

"The Motosas," said Dr. Cooper.

"Right."

"They've got some fields planted down there," Lila reported.

"Savages who farm?" Jay wondered.

Dr. Cooper took a long, careful look at the Stone's top. It appeared smooth enough to land on, although lightly frosted with ice. "Well, while we're up this high, I think we should check out that summit."

"*All right!*" said Jay.

Lila considered how the icy flat top of the stone ended at such a keen, straight edge, and how the vertical sides dropped almost two miles straight down. "Are you sure?"

Dr. Cooper eased the throttle back. The roar of the engine dropped in tone and the plane began to descend. "Everybody check your seat belt. We'll come in a bit high and do a flyover, just to feel how the wind is. If it feels right, we'll land."

He put the plane into a gentle turn, keeping the Stone's flat, rectangular surface in the windshield. So far the air was smooth, just like the top of the Stone.

"Oooh!" Dr. Henderson cried as the plane gave a lurch like an elevator going up.

"Updraft," Dr. Cooper said matter-of-factly. "The Stone's heating up the air around it. The air's rising, and we're in it. This could be a little sporty after all."

He pulled the throttle back to idle as they passed over the straight, sharp edge of the Stone. Suddenly they were no longer ten thousand feet above the ground; the surface of the Stone was only a few hundred feet below them, flat and featureless like the top of a monstrous desk, and lightly dusted with snow that looked like powdered sugar. The plane was bucking a little, tilting and fishtailing in turbulence.

Dr. Henderson cinched up her seat belt as tight as it would go. "I hope you know what you're doing!"

"Aw, this is nothing for Dad," said Jay.

They were less than a hundred feet off the surface. They could see wisps of powdery snow swirling in lacy shapes along the ground, which helped Dr. Cooper determine the direction of the wind.

"Couldn't ask for a wider runway," he said as he added a touch of flaps.

As Jay and Lila looked below, the shadow of the airplane grew larger and larger, coming up to meet them. Then it joined them as the tires chirped on the stone and ice. Dr. Henderson threw her head back and released a held breath.

"Okay," said Dr. Cooper as the plane slowed to a gentle stop, the tires skidding just a little on the powdery ice. "Let's get the work done and get off this thing before the winds kick up."

"We'll set out the sensors for the seismic experiment," said Dr. Henderson. "They're in that wooden crate in the back."

Stepping out onto the smooth, flat surface felt like stepping onto another planet. No desert, no dry lake bed, no other place on earth, could match the perfect, featureless flatness that stretched for miles. Nor was there ever a sight like the lacy wisps of powder-fine ice and snow floating steadily along in ghostly, numberless hordes only inches above the surface. The movement of the powdery ice and snow was so even, so constant, and so vast, that the Coopers and Dr. Henderson couldn't help but feel *they* were the ones moving. It was eerie, unnatural, and spooky. And none of them had forgotten that they were now walking directly on the back of the "sleeping lion."

The sensors were small, hand-sized transmitters designed to sense vibrations in the ground. Jay carried the wooden crate and Lila did the placing as they made a wide circle around the airplane according to Dr. Henderson's instructions. They were wearing oversized jackets borrowed from the Togwanan army, for at just under eleven thousand feet, the atmosphere was much cooler. Thinner, too. Just a short run could make them pant for air.

From where they stood, the airplane looked tiny and singular, like a gnat or a particle of dust resting on a tabletop. Beyond the airplane were almost four miles of laser-straight flat surface. The sight jarred the senses because it simply did not occur anywhere on the planet. Even the ocean on the calmest of days had a horizon because of the curvature of the earth. But the Stone did not curve out of sight in the distance—it just ended at a sheer, straight edge they could see in all directions. Jay was thrilled at the thought of hiking to the edge to look two miles straight down, but he knew there was work to do and little time.

KABOOM! Dr. Henderson's seismic blaster was like a small cannon held in a steel frame and aimed at the ground. When Jay pressed the detonator switch to set off the explosive charge, the device actually leaped a foot off the surface with Jay and Lila standing on it—supposedly to hold it down. Dr. Jennifer Henderson sat calmly in the shade of the airplane's wing, her jacket collar up around her face to block the cold wind, tapping away at her portable computer.

"We should get an image in just a few seconds," she told Dr. Cooper, who was looking over her shoulder. "The blaster sends shock waves through the Stone, and the sensors pick up the echoes. Then the computer interprets the echoes to let us know where the shock waves have been, whether they've passed through rooms or tunnels or different strata of rock. . . ."

The tiny cursor was sweeping back and forth across the computer screen. Line by line, beginning at the top, it was weaving an image like a tapestry. So far the image was one solid field of black. Dr. Henderson started tapping some keys. "Come on, come on . . . don't disappoint me."

"Woo!" Jay hollered as he and Lila hurried back to the plane. "That blaster was some kind of ride!"

Lila was twisting her finger in her ear. "That thing hurt my ears!"

They joined Dr. Cooper and looked over Dr. Henderson's shoulder at the computer image. The black tapestry continued to form on the computer screen as she tapped a few more keys, muttering to herself and scolding the computer, "Come on, don't give me that!"

Finally, the seismic image was complete. Dr. Henderson leaned back, removed her hands from the keyboard, and sighed. "People, unless the equipment isn't working properly, I'm afraid the results are disappointing. The Stone is solid. No rooms, no tunnels, nothing."

"Nothing?" Jay asked, clearly disappointed.

Dr. Henderson shook her head, waving her finger over the image on the screen. "See here? Between the top and bottom surfaces there is virtually no change in density. No cracks. No holes. No gaps or bubbles. Nothing."

"So we haven't progressed much," said Dr. Cooper.

"We may have fallen back a little. We don't even know what the Stone is made of."

"But you said it was basalt," said Lila.

Dr. Henderson shot a glance at the gas-powered core drill lying next to the plane's wheel strut, the drill bit burned and blunted. "While you were setting out the sensors, I tried to drill out a core sample. The drill didn't even make a scratch. If I'm going to be scientific and objective here, I have to admit I don't know what this thing is or what it's made of. I only know it's indestructible."

"Do you still think it's man-made?" Dr. Cooper asked.

Jennifer Henderson sniffed a derisive little laugh. "I'm wondering what the builder used for a chisel. Even though he, or it, or they, left marks, *I* sure can't."

Lila turned her back to a cold breeze that had just kicked up. "His Excellency isn't going to like this."

"Just for my information," said Dr. Henderson, "now that we have the airplane, can't we just fly out of the country from here?"

Dr. Cooper looked across the vast, tabletop surface toward the distant horizon, barely visible beyond the Stone's sharp edge. "Yes, we can. I'm just not sure how far we can go on the fuel we have left."

"Far enough to get out of Togwana would be fine with me."

"But the question is, where can we go? If any of the neighboring countries help us escape, Nkromo would brand them as enemies. I'm not sure they'd want that."

"Well," said Lila, "at least we're safe up here."

As if in response to her words, a disturbing quiver came up through the soles of their shoes.

"I knew it," Dr. Henderson moaned.

The Stone was quaking, all right. Dr. Henderson's computer almost slid off its little stand before she grabbed it. The airplane began to rock, its wings dipping and jiggling. From deep below and all around, there was a deep rumble, like continuous thunder, as a gust of wind whipped across the Stone, kicking up tiny ice pellets that stung their faces.

Dr. Henderson was already throwing her gear into the plane. "Let's go, let's go!"

Dr. Cooper looked to the east and saw a curtain of snow, ice, and boiling clouds coming their way. "Fair weather's over. We'd better get off this thing!"

Lila looked the direction her father was looking and saw the storm approaching. Even so, she insisted, "But we're safe here, really!"

Dr. Cooper just tugged her toward the plane. "Jay, unchock the wheels!"

Dr. Henderson started running away and he grabbed her.

"I've got to get the blaster!" she yelled over the rumble and the wind. "And the drill, and all those sensors—"

"What about the *airplane?*" Dr. Cooper yelled back. "If it gets damaged, we'll never get down!"

The Stone lurched like a bucking horse. The airplane actually skipped backward several feet, and the Coopers tumbled to the ground. The wind began to whip at them angrily.

Dr. Henderson didn't need any more convincing. With a cry of fear, she struggled to her feet, jerked the door open, and clambered inside.

Jay and Lila jumped in the back, Dr. Cooper in the front. The plane was still dancing and side-stepping along the quivering ground as Dr. Cooper rattled off the checklist, his hands flying from lever to button to gauge to switch. "Fuel tanks both, electrical off, breakers in, prop on maximum, carb heat cold . . ."

He twisted the starter switch and the engine came to life, the prop spinning into a blurred disk in front of the windshield.

A blast of wind, snow, and ice hit them broadside from the right. The plane weather-vaned into it, the tail spinning wildly to the left.

"Okay, we're nose into the wind," said Dr. Cooper, jamming the throttle wide open.

The airplane lunged forward, the white swirls of

48

snow and ice blowing past them like sheets in the wind. The old Cessna bucked, skidded, swerved, and tilted as the wind tossed it about, slapping against it this way, then that way. It gained speed, began to tiptoe, then skip along the surface. Dr. Cooper eased the control yoke back, and it took to the air.

"Are we safe?" Dr. Henderson pleaded.

An angry burst of wind came up under one wing and almost flipped the plane over. "Not yet," said Dr. Cooper, trying to hold the plane steady.

Below them, the sharp edge of the Stone appeared to rotate, tilt, rise, and fall as the airplane was tossed about like a leaf in the wind. The Cessna roared, climbed, struggled, clawed for altitude. Another blast of wind carried it sideways.

"Dad, what is it?" Jay asked. "What's happening?"

"Heat-generated updrafts," he yelled over the roar of the engine. "Convergence, convection, wind shear, I don't know—the Stone's affecting the weather."

The plane lurched sideways, twisting, banking, creaking in every joint. A cloud of snow and ice boiled beneath them like an angry white ocean. Dr. Cooper turned the plane eastward, trying to climb above the storm. Below them, the east edge of the Stone came no closer. The wind was so strong they were standing still!

Then the edge of the Stone began to retreat from them. The wind was blowing them backward!

"Oh, brother," said Dr. Cooper.

"What?" Dr. Henderson cried.

"We're in for a ride. Hang on."

"Can't you do something?"

"If I try to fight against this turbulence, the plane will break apart! We just have to ride it out!"

He eased the throttle back to slow the airplane down, then turned it westward to fly with the wind and get clear of the Stone. The Stone was hidden now beneath an angry mantle of storm clouds, but they could see the clouds breaking over its western edge like water flowing over a waterfall.

"Wind shear," said Dr. Cooper.

"Oh, no," whined Dr. Henderson.

Suddenly, the clouds seemed to suck them down, and they dropped into a nether world of pure white cotton on all sides with no up, no down, no sense of direction.

The altimeter was spinning backward, and they could feel the pressure of the atmosphere building against their ears. Eleven thousand, said the altimeter. Ten thousand. Nine.

They were helpless in a violent downdraft, tossed, twisted, thrown about in the clouds.

Eight thousand. Seven. Six.

And there was nothing they could do, except pray.

FIVE

Dr. Cooper had only one course of action available to him, and that was to fly the plane—just keep it under control, keep it flying. The plane was being knocked all over the sky. They braced themselves against the walls of the cabin, the seats, the floor, and each other, and still the plane plummeted earthward. As clouds whipped past the windshield and the plane quivered with every new gust of wind, Jacob Cooper kept an iron hand on the control yoke and the throttle, watching the airspeed and altimeter and making no sudden moves.

They knew that the Stone had to be out there somewhere in all those boiling clouds, but just how close was it? A collision would be no contest.

"Dear Jesus," Lila prayed out loud, "we're in your hands."

Suddenly, light burst through the windows as they dropped out of the clouds into clear air.

"*Yes!*" Jay shouted.

They could see the ground, and it looked awfully close. But the altimeter was no longer winding down. The violent downdraft was contacting the ground and turning sideways, becoming a powerful wind.

But where was the Stone? Every head twisted left and right trying to find it.

"There it is!" Jay shouted. "Nine o'clock!"

They could see the huge wall, dark and ominous in the cloudy gray light, stretching from the earth into the clouds. It appeared to be at least a mile away, and the good news was that the wind had carried them away from the Stone, not toward it.

Just then, they saw grass roofs slipping quickly by below them. Cattle. People.

"The Motosa village!" said Jay. "We're right above it!"

The engine sputtered and coughed. "Well," said Dr. Cooper, fiddling with the knobs and ignition, "what do you know!"

"What?" asked Dr. Henderson.

"We've lost the engine."

"*What?*"

"Carburetor ice, I suppose, or a broken fuel line. Hang on. I'm setting up for a landing."

Dr. Cooper turned the plane into the wind and aimed for a stretch of flat ground. The gusty, unpredictable wind lifted the plane, then dropped it, then knocked it sideways. "Check your seat belts!"

By now, they couldn't get their seat belts any tighter.

The wind dropped suddenly and so did the plane, so abruptly they could feel it in their stomachs. The desert floor rushed up at them, only thirty feet below, then twenty, then ten. Dr. Cooper fought for control as sagebrush, grass, and stones raced by below the wheels.

WHAM! The wind slammed the plane into the ground. The wheels bounced, the plane floated up again, then fell again, the wheels digging into the soft earth, kicking up dust, gouging out ruts. Dr. Cooper pulled back on the control yoke to keep the plane from nosing over as it swerved, bucked, bounced, and rumbled over the ground.

IMPACT! The right wheel hit a large rock. The plane spun in a circle, tilting wildly, the left wingtip clipping the top of a bush. Then the right wheel strut gave way, and the plane collapsed to the ground in a cloud of dust.

And then it was over. The plane sat amid desert stones and scraggly, yellow grass. It was quiet and still now, one strut broken and the right wingtip resting on the ground.

Jay and Lila relaxed, sat up, and looked around, letting out an audible breath of relief.

Dr. Henderson was all folded up with her arms clamped around her head. Only after a long, uninterrupted moment of silence and stillness did she slowly, timidly unwrap herself and come up for a look.

Dr. Cooper still had one hand clamped around the control yoke as he went through his shut-down checklist, flipping switches, turning knobs, shifting levers. In seconds, the aircraft was secure. Then he rested back in his seat, relaxed for the first time in what seemed an eternity of terror, and prayed in a quiet voice, "Ohhh, thank you, Lord, for a safe landing!"

"Thank you, Lord," Lila agreed.

"Thaaaank *you*," said Jay.

"Well, you can sit here and pray if you want," said Dr. Henderson, "but *I'm* getting out of this plane!"

Click, clack, their seat belts came loose and they piled out the doors, Dr. Henderson and Jay having to duck under the drooping wing on the right side.

"OWW!" Dr. Henderson fell to the ground, grimacing in pain, her hand going to her knee.

Jay leaped to her side, followed by Lila and Dr. Cooper. "What is it?"

Jennifer Henderson was hurt and angry at the same time. "I hurt my leg! Dr. Cooper, you broke the plane and me with it!"

Dr. Cooper knelt beside her and helped her roll up her pantleg. Her knee was beginning to swell. "Can you move it at all?"

She lay on her back, her face crinkled in agony, and gave it a try. She could move it, but it hurt terribly.

Dr. Cooper checked the knee as she worked it. "Well, nothing's broken, but your knee is badly bruised."

Dr. Henderson let her head plop on the soft, sandy ground and wagged it in despair. "Why me? Why me?"

"But you're still alive," Lila offered. "And you're safe."

Boom, bubbaboom, buboom, buboom boom. The sound of African drums came floating to them on the wind.

"The Motosas," said Jay. "Their village can't be far from here."

Dr. Henderson gave Lila a despairing look. "I only wish I could run."

"The question is, where?" said Dr. Cooper, surveying the area all around them. The bare desert gave way to a dry, grassy plain with singular trees popping up here and there, but this was still open country and their wrecked airplane had to be visible for miles. "I have little doubt the Motosas know we're here. Those drums could be an alarm."

"Well, I say we try to get back to the other side."

"It would be difficult, if not impossible. The Stone's blocking the road, and those hills at either end would be a tough climb even if you weren't injured."

Dr. Henderson struggled to get up. "Well, I'm not staying here to become somebody's dinner!"

"Can you walk at all?" Dr. Cooper asked, lending his arm.

She put weight on the leg and nearly collapsed again, wincing at the pain. "OWW . . . no."

Dr. Cooper helped her get comfortable on the ground again, then ducked under the airplane's wing and reached inside the cabin.

"I'll try the plane's radio. Maybe we can contact somebody."

Boom boom buboom, the drums kept playing away.

"Do we have any weapons?" Dr. Henderson asked, sitting up.

Jay and Lila looked at each other for an answer.

"A few tools, maybe," said Jay. "A wrench, a screwdriver . . ."

"Rocks," Lila suggested.

Dr. Henderson smiled dryly, looking up at the sky. "I'm the luckiest woman in the world!"

Dr. Cooper tried several times to raise someone on the radio, but he couldn't get an answer. Finally, he set the microphone back in its holder and shut the radio off. "The Stone must be blocking our signal."

The wind had begun to die down as the storm ebbed away. The sun poked holes through the thinning clouds.

Boom boom buboom boom. The drums sounded louder.

Dr. Cooper scanned the countryside. "We've got to find some shelter, some place to hide."

"Dad!" Lila whispered. "I think I saw something!"

They all looked in the direction Lila pointed. To the north was an expansive plain of sagebrush and prairie grass, and beyond that, a thin, scraggly forest. Nothing seemed out of place and nothing moved except the grass in the breeze.

"I don't see anything," Jay said quietly.

"There's somebody out there," Lila insisted.

They noticed for the first time that the drumbeats had ceased. They heard nothing except the gentle hiss of the breeze through the dry grass.

But was the motion in the grass just from the breeze?

Dr. Cooper was the first to see a face emerge, painted with clay and camouflaged with blades of grass to make it nearly invisible against its surroundings. Slowly, with increasing boldness, the warrior rose from his hiding place in the tall grass to his full height, brandishing a spear in one hand, ready to hurl it at the slightest wrong move.

Lila came alongside her father and held him tightly as another warrior appeared, and then another, each one painted from head to foot to look just like the prairie, like he was made of earth and grass. To the north, and then to the west, and now from the south, more warriors appeared as if growing out of the ground, springing up like cornstalks in a time-lapse movie. It was remarkable how close they'd gotten without being detected.

"They're very good," said Dr. Cooper.

The warriors came out into the clear, moving stealthily, catlike, their feet touching lightly, silently on the ground. With precision and discipline, they formed a circle, evenly spaced like fenceposts, around the airplane and its occupants, their spears ready. Jacob Cooper counted about thirty. They were not naked, but close to it, dressed for a hunt and dead serious about it. Their expressions were grim through all the mud and grass camouflage.

Dr. Cooper raised his hand very slowly, making sure they could see it was empty, and then gave a slight wave of greeting. "Hello."

Some of the warriors directly in front of Dr. Cooper finally spoke, but not to him. They were looking at the broken airplane, pointing, muttering to each other, and even getting excited. They called to some other warriors who hurried over to confer in a tight huddle. Word began to travel around the circle, and now everyone seemed excited. Two warriors ran back into the grass, apparently to spread the word to the rest of the village, whatever the word was. Those who remained began to stare at Dr. Cooper, pointing at him, discussing him among themselves.

"I'm Dr. Jacob Cooper—"

Twenty-eight arms raised spears. The warriors were fascinated with Jacob Cooper, but still wary of him.

"Dad . . ." Jay whispered and then pointed to the north.

The two messengers were returning, bounding through the grass with the grace and agility of gazelles, and behind them, marching with quick, deliberate steps, were four men and . . . a bush. At least that's what it looked like from a distance— some kind of bizarre plant sticking above the prairie grass with leaves, grass, and even a few small tree branches arranged like a walking flower arrangement. From the way the warriors quieted down and shuffled sideways to make room, this had to be someone important approaching.

The "bush" came closer, and at last they could see a grim, black face in the center of an elaborate headdress of fur and foliage.

Dr. Henderson drew a surprised breath.

Lila gasped right along with Dr. Henderson and then whispered, "Dad, is that Mr. Mobutu?"

Dr. Cooper kept watching as the very important person came closer. At first glance, and from a distance, the man did bear a remarkable resemblance to

Nkromo's chief secretary, but with a second look it was easy to tell, "No, it isn't Mobutu. I believe this is the tribal chief, the man who holds our lives in his hands."

The chief walked briskly into the circle with authority in every step and an ornately carved staff in his hand. He was attended by four men dressed in woven tunics and elaborate belts and sashes of grass and bark—uniforms, obviously, the proper attire for attendants to the tribal chief. As for the chief, besides the towering headdress, he also wore a breastplate of woven bones and bark, a breathtaking sash of crafted leather, leather sandals with bindings that wound up his legs to his knees, and, as the ultimate symbol of power and high office, a genuine pair of jogging shorts with the word *Nike* clearly embossed on the leg.

What might have happened to the former owner of those shorts was something they tried not to think about.

Dr. Cooper gave a slight bow, as did Jay and Lila. Dr. Henderson, still seated on the ground, bowed as best she could.

The chief came forward and eyed Dr. Cooper carefully as some of his warriors whispered counsel to him, pointing at the airplane, gesturing at Dr. Cooper. The chief seemed to agree with whatever they were telling him, and the more they talked, the more alarmed he looked. Finally, he spoke to Dr. Cooper, pointing and giving instructions in the Motosa language.

His words meant nothing, of course, and the

Coopers and Dr. Henderson could only exchange blank looks.

The chief grew impatient, and repeated the order, pointing at Jacob Cooper's head. Dr. Cooper raised his hand and touched his hat. The chief nodded. Dr. Cooper removed his hat and held it in his hand.

There was an audible gasp from the circle of warriors and the chief cocked his head, his face full of wonder.

"Looks like you're in the spotlight," Dr. Henderson said quietly.

"So what do I do to perform?" Dr. Cooper asked.

"English!" the chief exclaimed. "You speak English!"

Dr. Cooper wanted to feel relieved. Was this a good sign? "Uh . . . yes, I do."

"Who are you?"

"Dr. Jacob Cooper, from America. And this is my daughter Lila, and that is my son Jay. And this is Dr. Jennifer Henderson, also from America."

The chief broke into a wide smile, then laughed with joy. Then he bellowed a loud announcement to his warriors. They erupted in cheers, waving their spears in the air, smiling, laughing, hopping up and down.

Dr. Cooper just smiled at them as he quietly told Dr. Henderson and the kids, "Well, we've done *something* to please them."

"Maybe they just heard tonight's menu," Dr. Henderson whispered.

Then Dr. Cooper asked the chief, "Are you the Motosas?"

"Yes, yes!" replied the chief. "Motosas, yes!" He stepped forward, all smiles, all joy. "You come! Come to village! You talk! We hear!"

Before the Coopers understood what was happening, four men locked their arms together to form a chair and lifted Dr. Cooper off the ground like some kind of football hero. Four others did the same for Dr. Henderson, while two pairs of men carried Jay and Lila. With a majestic wave of his staff, the chief led the parade, and, breaking into a song, they headed across the grassy plain.

It was an odd feeling, being carried along by these cheering, mud-painted savages. Jay and Lila tried to smile and act pleased, but they'd heard stories about savage tribes who went to great lengths to win friends just so they could betray and eat them later. Dr. Cooper had heard the same stories and was trying to remember if he'd heard them from Brent Anderson, who had worked in this country.

The parade passed over gently rolling prairie land, through waist-high grass, and past lone, aged trees. At last the Coopers caught sight of the thatched rooftops of the village on the edge of a forest. The trail took them under the sheltering canopy of the trees and then into the center of the village. There chickens and goats scattered out of their path and women and children stopped to stare and wonder at the commotion.

The warriors called to their wives, pointed at the Coopers, and rattled off rapid, excited explanations. The women grew wide-eyed and clapped their hands in awe, chattering among themselves and calling to their children. The main thoroughfare through the village was coming alive with men, women, and children, all gathering and babbling and clapping their hands as they followed the parade.

The Coopers and Dr. Henderson just let themselves be carried along through the village, observing the well-built, multi-roomed, pole and grass structures, watering troughs for the animals carved from whole logs, inventive, hand-woven garments, and intricate jewelry made from stones, bones, and leather.

The thoroughfare opened into a large village square where chickens scratched about and children kicked and chased a furry, fuzzy ball in some kind of team sport. In the center of the square was a well. It was enclosed with a circular wall of stones and topped with a beam from which a bucket could be lowered. At the far end of the square was a large, tent-like structure with a thatched roof but no walls. Beyond that, fields of corn and wheat struggled to survive in the dry climate.

The parade carried the Coopers and Dr. Henderson right up to the big tent-like structure as two musicians started pounding big drums as a clarion call. In response, the rest of the villagers began to gather from the fields, from the huts, and from the dry prairie beyond, chattering with curiosity and excitement.

The men carrying the Coopers set them down gently; the men carrying Dr. Henderson continued to carry her under the big roof. The chief extended his big, powerful arm inside. "Please! Come! We sit! We hear!"

The Coopers followed the chief inside, past rows of log benches arranged in theater-like fashion, to an open area in the front where a large, flat stone served as a one-man platform.

"Wow," Jay whispered to Lila. "If I didn't know we were in a primitive African village, I'd think we were in an old revival tent!"

Lila nodded, smiling at the similarity. "It must be their meeting hall."

Dr. Henderson was already seated comfortably on a log bench in the very front, wincing just a bit as a gray-haired man in a bone necklace and grass skirt examined her knee, nodding and muttering to an assistant or apprentice who nodded and muttered back. This was apparently the village witch doctor.

"It's fine, really," Dr. Henderson protested. "I don't need any spells cast on me, thank you."

The chief motioned for the Coopers to stand beside the stone platform while the people swarmed in from every direction, filling the log benches, chattering, and staring at the Coopers with wonder.

The chief stepped onto the stone and raised his arms to signal for quiet. The place quieted down immediately. He addressed them all in a voice that did not need a microphone or loudspeakers. And he appeared to be introducing the strangers who stood there, still oblivious to what was going on.

Then the chief looked down from his stone platform and grinned at Dr. Cooper. The people grinned, too, snickering with delight. The chief pointed to Dr. Cooper's head, bellowed another few sentences, and then, before Dr. Cooper could resist or react, he reached over and rubbed his fingers furiously through Dr. Cooper's hair. That being done, he stepped back and held out his hands toward Dr. Cooper's tousled head as if to say, "Voilà!"

The people seemed to understand the point. They rose to their feet, laughing, cheering, pointing, nodding, clapping.

"Speech! Speech!" Jay cheered, clapping along, which earned him another corrective poke from Lila.

The chief offered Dr. Cooper his big hand and yanked him up onto the stone. The crowd sat down, and the place got quiet.

"You talk," said the chief. "We hear, yes!"

Then the chief sat down on the front log and waited expectantly with all the others.

Dr. Cooper looked out at all those faces looking back and felt stark naked. What in the world were they expecting him to say? What was he supposed to do? He caught a look from Dr. Henderson. She wasn't saying it out loud, but her eyes sent the message clear enough: "Doctor, you really *are* in the spotlight now!"

The warriors who had brought them here still had their spears in their hands and were eyeing him warily.

Hoo boy, he thought. *If they don't like whatever speech I come up with, we could all be Cooper soup!*

And still the people waited.

SIX

Um . . ." Dr. Cooper cleared his throat and gave the people a smile he hoped they would like. "Uh, on behalf of my children and my colleague, Dr. Henderson, I bid you greetings."

Jay and Lila, still standing on the ground in front of the platform, gave a little wave, hoping that would help convey their dad's meaning.

The chief stood up to look for someone and finally caught the eye of the gray-haired witch doctor who had been looking at Dr. Henderson's knee. The chief jerked his head toward Dr. Cooper and the man hurried over and leaped up on the rock, offering his hand. "I am Bengati! Welcome."

Dr. Cooper was relieved to find another English speaker in the group. "Dr. Jacob Cooper. You know English, then?"

"My father was a guide for white hunters. He learned the language, and taught it to me. I have taught the chief and his family, but . . ." He shrugged. "When there is no need to speak it, it is hard for them to remember."

Bengati immediately introduced Dr. Jacob

Cooper to the crowd. Dr. Cooper picked up his cue and introduced his children and Dr. Henderson, and Bengati interpreted again.

The chief spoke several sentences. Bengati interpreted, "Our Chief welcomes you and says the people have gathered to hear whatever it is you have to say."

Dr. Cooper confided in a lowered voice, "I'm not really sure what I'm *supposed* to say. Is there—"

Bengati interpreted Dr. Cooper's confidence to the crowd before he could stop him, and everyone exchanged puzzled looks.

Dr. Cooper hurried to say, "But, uh, we are scientists from America, and we have come here to study this vast, mysterious stone that has appeared in the desert."

The people fell silent and serious when Bengati told them that, nodding their heads, their eyes glued on Dr. Cooper.

The chief asked a question.

"The chief and the people want to know, what does the stone mean?" Bengati interpreted.

"Mean?" That question caught Dr. Cooper by surprise. "Uh, well, we're not sure what it means. We've only just arrived and as you know, encountered some trouble with our airplane. We're not even sure where the Stone came from, or how it got here."

When Bengati delivered that answer, Jay and Lila could see it didn't please the crowd at all. In perfect unison, all those awestruck, expectant faces changed to disappointment.

The chief wasn't very happy either. He fired another question, his voice a little more stern.

Bengati interpreted, "You really do not know how it got here?"

"Uh . . . no, not yet."

The chief rose to his feet, exasperated, shaking his head and waving his arms as if trying to erase the whole event. He bellowed an announcement to the crowd, and everyone stood up and started to leave.

"The meeting is over," Bengati told the Coopers. "You did not answer the chief's questions correctly."

"You could have *made up* something," Dr. Henderson muttered.

The chief stepped up to Dr. Cooper, still shaking his head, and made a simple statement.

Bengati interpreted, "Have you no eyes? *God* put it there."

Lila's mouth dropped open. She shot a triumphant glance at Dr. Henderson. The geologist merely sneered.

The chief continued to speak while Bengati interpreted. "We hoped you would teach us, but now *we* must teach *you*."

The chief gave some quick orders to his warriors and stomped from the building, obviously angry and disappointed.

The warriors moved forward and surrounded them again, pushing Bengati to the outside of the circle. The warrior in charge shook his spear and shouted, gesturing toward the village. Bengati called from across the crowd, "You are to go with those men now."

Four warriors got their arms locked under Dr.

Henderson and picked her up, but there were no such seats for the Coopers.

They had to walk, guided by the points of spears.

"Well, it seems our popularity has lagged," said Dr. Cooper.

"Face it, Cooper, you bombed," said Dr. Henderson.

Surrounded tightly on all sides and led by armed warriors, they left the meeting hall and went out into the village square as the crowd continued to disperse. Some returned to their homes, others back into the fields, and several back to the open prairie, disappearing over a low rise. The formidable Stone filled the sky beyond them.

"What do cannibals do?" Lila asked. "I mean . . . do they just throw you into a big soup pot or what?"

Dr. Cooper touched her. "Lila, don't give in to thoughts like that."

Jay sniffed. "Hey. Smells like a barbecue."

"Of course," said Dr. Henderson. "And guess who the main course is going to be!"

Jacob Cooper's voice was firm. "Dr. Henderson, I'll thank you to control such outbursts!"

"Sorry." Her tone said she wasn't.

They seemed to be going toward the smell, marching up a narrow path that wound between the grass huts and beneath the sheltering limbs of ancient trees. When they rounded the last corner, they beheld a sight that made them stare. At the end of the path was a special grass hut, built in and around a massive tree so that the roof timbers were suspended from the tree's lower limbs.

"Now *this* is different," said Jay.

"It's like something out of Peter Pan!" said Lila, captivated. "Where the Lost Boys live!"

The warriors led them up to the front door and halted there in a neat formation. There was a shout and the tribal chief, now without his ornate head-dress, emerged from his house and stood before his door, his expression grim, his fists on his hips.

"Ben-ga-ti!" he hollered.

Bengati shouted in acknowledgment as he came running from behind the crowd.

The chief thundered a few sentences as Bengati came alongside to interpret. "The chief wishes to have you as his guests for dinner."

The Coopers and Dr. Henderson exchanged glances. Now just what did he mean by that?

The warriors all bowed slightly and turned away, heading back down the path into the village. The only ones who remained were Bengati and those bearing Jennifer Henderson.

"Come," said the chief, gesturing with his big arms, "You come. Come eat."

Dr. Henderson went first—she had no choice, as the warriors carried her gently through the narrow door. Dr. Cooper, Jay, and Lila followed behind. Their eyes darted everywhere, alert for knives in hands, warriors waiting in ambush, any sign of danger.

Inside the chief's hut, they saw dinner already prepared, laid out in banquet style on a low, rough-hewn table. In the center of the table, surrounded by meticulous arrangements of fruits and vegetables, was a huge roast pig, still hot and crackling, just off the spit.

They were going to *eat* dinner, not *be* dinner.

Their relief was so obvious the chief asked through Bengati, "Are you all right? Is something wrong with the food?"

Dr. Cooper waved his hand and shook his head and even chuckled with relief. "No, no, everything's wonderful. The roast pig is . . . it's a wonderful sight to see!"

"Fabulous!" Dr. Henderson agreed, still drawing deep breaths so she could sigh with relief, her hand over her heart.

The chief introduced his family: a beautiful wife with coal black skin and a smooth, sculptured face—"She is Renyata"; a handsome, athletic son just a little older than Jay—"He is my son, Ontolo"; and a beautiful daughter about Lila's age with long, intricate braids—"She is Beset." Then he thumped his chest and announced proudly, "And I am Gotono! I am chief!"

The Coopers and Dr. Henderson bowed in greeting and respect as they shook hands with each of Chief Gotono's family. Jay and Ontolo hit it off immediately and even exchanged a few small gifts. Then, at the chief and Renyata's invitation—and with the four warriors assisting Dr. Henderson—they took their places around the table, sitting on the floor on a comfortable woven mat of straw. The chief extended his hand over the table while he pronounced some kind of blessing, and they started eating. It felt just like family dinner on a Sunday afternoon.

As they ate, the chief spoke and Bengati interpreted. "I apologize for the embarrassment we caused you. You were not who we expected." Before they could figure out what that was supposed to mean, the chief kept right on going. "But now you are guests here with us, and we welcome you."

"Thank you," said Dr. Cooper. "And we apologize that we did not meet your expectations."

Bengati relayed the message in Motosa and the chief laughed. "So you have come to learn of the Stone," he answered through Bengati. "The Stone is a work of our god, but it is a great mystery. We do not know what our god intends by placing it there. We do not yet know its meaning. That is why we asked *you*."

Dr. Henderson got bold. "Well, if you don't know the meaning of the Stone, then how can you be sure your god put it there?"

The Coopers tensed a bit at that question, afraid it would cause offense, but the chief only nodded in approval and gave his answer.

"That is a fair question," Bengati translated.

The chief reached over and took his long, ornately carved staff from its place in the corner. He held it up for all to see, and ran his fingers over the carvings of animals, birds, and trees. Bengati relayed his words, "If you were to happen upon this staff in the middle of the desert, you would think another man left it there. You would not think it suddenly appeared for no reason. And why is that? Because anyone can see it is created. It is carved by a maker's hand. So the Stone is the same way. It is no ordinary stone. It is created by the hand of a craftsman, the hand of our god."

Dr. Cooper could feel Lila's smile before he even looked to see it. He smiled back and threw her a wink.

The chief was continuing. "Our god does nothing without a reason, and soon we will know what the reason is. But this we do know: The Stone will bring us water for our crops, just as it has brought us you. This was all meant to be."

"Water for their crops?" Dr. Henderson wondered out loud.

Dr. Cooper caught her eye, and her meaning. "Sounds geological, doesn't it?"

Dr. Henderson turned to the chief. "You say the Stone will bring you water? How?"

The chief was delighted by the question. "The day is coming to an end. Tomorrow morning, you will see."

After dinner, the Coopers and Dr. Henderson were taken to a large home facing the village square. Like most homes in this village, it was a well-built, sod and grass, post and beam structure that rested on stone footings with a covered porch. The owner was an older woman with a round, jolly face.

"This is Jo-Jota," said Bengati, "a widow of three years and mother of five who are now grown. She has room inside for strangers, and you can all stay here."

"Wow," said Dr. Henderson, "Jo-Jota's boarding house."

"You may stay here in our village while you try to learn the secret of the Stone," the chief said as

Bengati interpreted. Then he looked at Dr. Henderson. "And we will care for you until your leg has healed."

She shook the chief's hand and replied, "Thank you, sir. We are indebted to you."

Dr. Cooper took Jo-Jota's offered hand in greeting. "We deeply appreciate your hospitality."

"Tomorrow," said the chief, "we will see the Stone together, and you will learn how the Stone will bring us water."

When morning came to the Motosa village, there was a strange, overcast dimness about it, as if the sun had come up, but not really. When Lila stepped onto Jo-Jota's porch to stretch and breathe the cool, morning air, she found her brother and father already observing how the Stone had affected the morning light.

"We're still in the Stone's shadow," said Jay.

"The desert, the grasslands, the village," Dr. Cooper observed, looking east, then west, "a lot of the forest, too, is all in the shadow. The sunlight won't break over the top edge of the Stone until midmorning."

Jo-Jota brought them a breakfast of wheat kernels mixed with raisins, which reminded them of granola, and goat's milk. They had just finished their meal when Chief Gotono, Bengati, and four warriors arrived, all smiles. The chief had appointed himself their official guide and had come to take them on a tour around the village.

The Coopers walked while Jennifer Henderson rode in style in a special chair carried by the four warriors. She griped a little bit, complaining that she was not a cripple, but the Coopers could tell she was actually enjoying herself.

Bengati tried to keep up with the translating as Chief Gotono rattled on and on like a tour guide. The chief pointed out new huts that had been built in a special expansion project for new sons- and daughters-in-law. Next he showed them the recently improved village well. Because of the recent dry years, it was now dug out twice as deep as it had been originally. Then he took them to the sheep and goat corrals, now with dwindling populations due to the loss of grazing land. From there they went to see the spinning and weaving projects that provided clothing, blankets, and household linens. Last, the chief showed them the fields of corn and wheat that were necessary for survival and yet sparse for lack of water.

"But that will change soon," he added.

They passed through the village heading eastward, toward the desert and toward the Stone. As they came from under the wide canopy of the trees and started to cross the open prairie, they could once again see the Stone stretching across the golden horizon and filling the sky like the biggest red barn ever made.

Lila admired the reddish color that seemed so deep on the shaded, western face of the Stone. It seemed to glow around its edges where the hidden sun's rays shot outward like the spokes of a huge wheel. "It's beautiful, isn't it?"

Dr. Cooper studied the Stone's distant outline and quietly asked his children, "Why aren't we afraid of it?"

Jay thought the question a little odd. "Are we supposed to be?"

"Well, come on: It's popped into existence out of nowhere; it's indestructible; it cuts the day in half; it quakes; and we got the scare of our lives in that storm it caused."

Jay considered that. "Well, we're okay now. Nothing really bad happened."

"The people on the other side are afraid of it."

"I've *never* been afraid of it," said Lila.

"And neither have I," said Jay.

"But why not?" their father pressed.

"I don't know," said Lila. "It'd be like being afraid of a sunset, or a beautiful mountain, or a whole forest turning golden in the fall. It's beautiful, and God made it, that's all I know."

"Yeah," Jay agreed. "I think Lila and the chief are right: God put it there."

Dr. Cooper nodded. "Which really makes me curious: What is it about a huge rock that draws such a response from us?"

"Well, what about the Motosas?" Jay asked. "They must be feeling the same thing. I mean, all those people on the other side—Nkromo, Mobutu, the soldiers—they think the Stone's a *boloa-kota,* and they're afraid of it. But the Motosas are glad the thing's here; they think their god sent it."

"Now *that* was interesting, to be sure," said Dr. Cooper. "I'd like to know more about the religious system here. They apparently believe in a creator, in one god."

"And they aren't cannibals, either," said Jay. "I don't know what Mr. Mobutu was talking about."

"Wow!" Lila said suddenly.

They were coming over a rise and could see the vast golden prairie in front of them. Where it faded into the desolate desert basin, the Stone, as solid, immovable, and mysterious as ever, towered above like a pillar holding up the sky. But now they had a new sight to behold.

At least fifty men, women, and children were laboring in a long, straight line, swinging picks and shovels, throwing the stubborn dirt out of a ditch that reached better than a mile across the prairie, into the desert, and to the base of the Stone. It was a marvelous accomplishment considering the primitive tools they were using—no backhoes or bulldozers here, only picks, shovels, muscles, and determination.

The chief was proud of the project, that was easy to see. He traced the path of the ditch in a long, flowing gesture and said with Bengati translating: "For years our life has been hard for lack of water. Our crops have struggled, our well has dropped lower and lower. But now, water will come. It will flow through this ditch from the Stone to our village."

Jennifer Henderson rose awkwardly in her chair and strained to see the farthest limits of the ditch. "But where is the water?"

"It will come," the chief replied.

He continued on, and they followed, hiking along

the ditch through the prairie and into the desert, getting closer and closer to the Stone. Dr. Henderson became visibly nervous again, but the men carrying her actually seemed to be excited for the opportunity to come this close to the Stone.

The Coopers continued to inspect the ditch as they walked along, until it came at last to a sudden stop at the northwest corner of the Stone.

Here, almost as a courtesy, the Stone allowed access to its corner over flat desert ground. Only a few hundred feet away, the Stone was jammed up against the sheer, rocky cliffs, barring any approach to the rest of its north surface as well as denying any passage to the other side. The Coopers and Dr. Henderson had never been to one of the Stone's corners. They'd never touched one or measured its angle, never placed their hands on the keen edge that shot straight up, true as a laser, into the upper reaches of the sky.

Dr. Cooper got there first, and with an excitement that he made no effort to conceal, he touched the corner. He ran his hand up and down it, sighted along the Stone's west face with one eye, then the Stone's north face, then carefully measured the angle formed where the two surfaces met.

"Incredible!" he exclaimed, so excited there was laughter in his voice. "Ninety degrees! Perfectly formed!"

Jennifer Henderson fidgeted in her chair and urged her carriers on. "Come on, get me over there!"

They carried her to the corner where she did the very same things Dr. Cooper had done, her breath quickening with excitement, her face filled with awe.

Jay and Lila took their turn, sighting up the corner, marveling at the dead-straight line and the perfectly square angle.

"Oh, Lord," Dr. Cooper found himself praying, *"what is it? What does it mean?"*

But now Dr. Henderson was carefully surveying the ground and the rocky strata the ditch had cut through. "Dr. Cooper. I don't think I have any good news for us or the Motosas. There's nothing here to indicate any kind of water table or aquifer."

The Motosas standing nearby did not fully understand her words, but they could understand her somber tone. They fell silent, wanting to know what she was saying.

"So you're saying . . . ?" Dr. Cooper asked.

"I'm saying there is no water here," she replied.

The chief seemed to understand what she was saying and touched her arm. Then he spoke, and Bengati translated. "You see with only one set of eyes and see only what is, not what can be."

Dr. Henderson didn't want to argue with their host. "I suppose that's right," she agreed. Then she muttered to Dr. Cooper, "I suppose *he* can predict what the geological forces will do next."

Then Chief Gotono turned to Jay and Lila with a sparkle in his eye. Bengati translated as the chief asked them, "Do *you* see with other eyes? Do you see the water flowing to our village?"

Well, of course they didn't, but they thought they understood his meaning.

Jay ventured, "You're, uh, digging this ditch in faith?"

Bengati wasn't sure how to interpret that.

Lila tried, "It's like a dream, a vision. You don't see any water, but still you believe it will be here."

Bengati interpreted that to the chief, and the chief laughed a deep, thunderous laugh that echoed off the Stone so clearly it sounded like a second man laughing right next to them. "Yes!" He thumped his heart. "In here, I know."

SEVEN

Back on Jo-Jota's porch, the chief and Bengati sat with the Coopers and Dr. Henderson. They were enjoying one of Jo-Jota's fruit juice concoctions as they rested from the day's heat.

The chief spoke, and as always, Bengati translated his words. "I know there is no water in the ditch. I know that no water can be seen. But do you see that well?" The chief pointed to the village well in the middle of the square. "Long ago, when there was no village, our ancestors came to this place. Their chief said, 'This is where we will live.' His people said, 'We cannot live here, there is no water.' But the chief had found a special stone upon the ground, and when he struck it with his staff, water came from beneath it. That water has been there ever since, and that is where our well is today. We are here, and our village is here, because long ago, a chief saw there would be water where once there was none."

Dr. Cooper smiled. The tale reminded him of Moses in the wilderness, striking a rock to bring forth water for the children of Israel. "In our culture, we have a story like that."

"So are you going to strike the Stone as your ancestor did?" Dr. Henderson asked.

The chief looked just a little awkward. "I have already done that, even before we dug the ditch."

Dr. Henderson couldn't hide the fact that she was troubled about all this. "But still you believe there will be water?"

"There is water there," the chief insisted. "Our well is going down. We have dug it deeper, but it is difficult to draw any more water from it. We have tried digging other wells, but cannot dig deep enough through the rock. If the Stone does not bring us water, we will perish. Our god would not let that happen."

Dr. Henderson said nothing and looked toward the square. Dr. Cooper could see she felt sorry for these people. "Dr. Henderson, what about the well these people have now? Doesn't that indicate the presence of water down there, some kind of aquifer?"

She weighed that and finally nodded. "Certainly. There are hills and mountains on all sides of the desert. Cracks and fissures under the ground could carry the rainwater from those hills into a vast reservoir under the desert floor. But even if there was water down there, you heard the chief: It's lying under solid rock and too far down for these people to reach it." She added glumly, her voice quiet and secretive. "And a two-foot-wide ditch across the desert isn't going to make much of a difference."

Dr. Cooper shot a glance over the thatched

rooftops of the village and through the trees. He could see the Stone still glistening in the afternoon sun. "Unless something really unusual happened," he offered.

She gazed at the Stone and shook her head fearfully. "You mean something *cataclysmic*. Doctor, any geological event big enough to break open that aquifer would probably wipe out this village in the process. I'd rather not think about that."

Just then, the chief's wife, Renyata, came around the corner with her son, Ontolo, and everyone could see that something was wrong. Renyata looked angry, and Ontolo walked with his head drooping, looking glum.

Renyata spoke quietly to Bengati, who relayed her words to the Coopers. "Renyata would like to know if you're missing a marking stick and some strange skin."

Renyata held up a pencil and some sheets of paper and spoke as Bengati translated. "It is against our ways for anyone to take something that belongs to another. It is the command of our god that we do not steal but work to produce what we desire and then share." She glanced briefly at her son. "I am afraid that my son Ontolo has been bitten by the snake and has done wrong."

Ontolo stood timidly, his eyes awaiting Jay's answer.

Jay was quite dismayed that Ontolo was in trouble. "Ma'am . . ." Jay knew he was about to contradict the chief's wife and tried to do it carefully. "Ontolo did not steal from me." He looked to Lila for her agreement. "I gave that pencil and paper to Ontolo as a gift when we first met yesterday." He reached into his pocket and brought out a crude knife. "And Ontolo gave me this knife. We're friends."

"That's right," said Lila. "It was a trade."

Bengati was only too happy to relay this to Renyata.

When she heard Jay's words, her grim expression melted. She looked embarrassed as she asked a question in halting English, "The pencil is . . . gift . . . to my Ontolo?"

Jay reached into his pocket and brought out another pencil. "Yes. And please, here is one for you as well."

She received the pencil from Jay's hand and looked at it in wonder. Then she put her arm around her son, and it was easy to see she was apologizing. Their faces brightened, they started smiling, and then, in a purposeful gesture, Renyata put both pencils into Ontolo's hand. "Thank you, Jay Cooper. Thank you for pencils." She looked to Bengati who translated the rest of her words. "I will give them both to my son, Ontolo, because he will know what to do with them."

Then the four Motosas laughed together at some private joke as Chief Gotono rose and gave his son a playful hug. "Come. We eat in my house."

Lunch was delightful, but Ontolo could hardly wait to be excused from the table and to pull Jay with him. The big tree Gotono's house was built around also served as a handy staircase to Ontolo's second story loft, and Ontolo led the way, clambering up the trunk while Jay followed.

Jay had to marvel, even chuckle a bit, at the sight of Ontolo's little room. It seemed very much like a primitive version of Jay's room back home. Instead of posters, skates, balls, and sports trophies, it was decorated with Ontolo's trophies: animal skins; brilliant bird feathers; a cane flute; a colorful, feathered spear; and an impressive breastplate made from leather and bones.

But Ontolo had something specific he wanted Jay to see, and he drew his friend's attention to a corner of the room where pieces of flattened tree bark and the stretched hides of small animals were stacked like schoolbooks on a small table. Ontolo picked up a piece of the bark, a flat, smooth surface about eight inches across, and put it in Jay's hand.

Jay looked at the piece of bark, not knowing what to expect. When he saw the bark was covered with tiny, orderly shapes and squiggles in neat rows, he took more than a second look. These were not just picture symbols or crude depictions of animals and adventures. The small, delicate scratches made with a sharp stick and the dark juice of berries had an unmistakable purpose.

Writing!

Jay pointed at the piece of bark in his hand and asked, "Did Ontolo do this?"

Ontolo nodded happily and immediately showed him a piece of skin stretched over a vine hoop. More writing. Ontolo pointed at the first character and indicated the sound it represented: "Oh." Then the next character and its sound: "Nnnn." Then the next: "Tuh." Then came "Oh," followed by "Llll," and finally, "Oh" again.

Jay pointed at the characters and sounded out the word himself. It was easy. "On-to-lo."

Ontolo got so excited that Jay feared he would fall out of the loft and onto the dinner guests below. "Ontolo!" he shouted, pointing at the word on the skin and then at himself. "Ontolo!"

"Yes," Jay nodded, realizing what he was seeing. "Ontolo. Your name."

"Ontolo is . . ." Ontolo looked around the room until his eyes lighted on the trunk of the big tree that held up the house. He tapped it with his fingers.

Jay tried to figure out what Ontolo was saying. "Ontolo is a tree?"

Ontolo shook his head, laughing at Jay's slowness in catching on. He tapped his chest with both hands. "Ontolo: My name is man . . ." But he couldn't think of the next word in English and tapped the trunk again.

"Man of tree?" Jay guessed.

Ontolo half-nodded and crinkled his face.

"Man of the tree?"

Ontolo only shrugged, not quite satisfied. "Man of the tree. Yes."

Ontolo took the skin from Jay and then, with one of the pencils Jay had given him, wrote two more characters and gave it back. "You see?" He pointed at the first character and made the sound it represented, "Juh."

Jay guessed the sound of the second character. "Ay."

Ontolo nodded, pleased with his pupil's progress.

Jay read the whole word. "Jay."

Ontolo laughed, totally pleased with how well this was working.

Jay pointed at the other skins and pieces of bark, all covered with Ontolo's strange marks. "Ontolo, you made all this?"

Ontolo was jubilant. "Yes. Ontolo make, in here!" He tapped his head, indicating it was all his own idea.

Jay was stunned. "Ontolo," he said, putting the skin back in Ontolo's hand, "write what I say."

Ontolo didn't fully understand, so Jay made motions toward his own mouth and then tapped on the skin and pointed at Ontolo's pencil. "Write: *i.*" The *i* sound Jay made was like the *i* in *big*. Jay tapped the skin again. "Write it."

"*Eee?*" Ontolo asked.

Jay nodded. "Close enough."

Ontolo shrugged and made a small mark.

"Now write *Nnn.*"

Ontolo formed another character, greatly enjoying the feel of the new pencil.

Jay made the sound of *Th,* and Ontolo made a face. He had no mark to represent that sound.

"Well how about *Tuh?*" Jay asked.

Ontolo nodded and scribbled. That would work.

Back in the main room, where the grown-ups visited and Beset was teaching Lila how to weave a beautiful headdress, Dr. Cooper looked up toward the loft where the two boys had been hiding out for quite some time. "It's awfully quiet up there."

Chief Gotono and Bengati laughed together at a private joke, and then the chief explained through Bengati, "I think Ontolo is playing with the pencils. He likes to draw and make funny marks."

"Jay?" Dr. Cooper called.

"Dad!" came Jay's answer as he swung from the loft to the trunk of the tree and started climbing down. "Dad, you've got to see this!"

"See what?"

Both boys came climbing, almost sliding, down the tree, full of excitement. Dr. Cooper had to wonder what was brewing, but the chief didn't seem too alarmed or curious; apparently his kids were always excited about something.

Jay landed on the floor and waited for Ontolo to drop down behind him. "Dad, you won't believe this! It's history, happening right here!"

Chief Gotono looked puzzled and Bengati tried to explain what was going on, though no one in the room really knew.

Jay took the skin from Ontolo and showed it to his father. "Look at this! It's a written alphabet!"

Dr. Cooper's eyes narrowed as he studied the weird little marks. Dr. Henderson hobbled over for a closer look. "An alphabet," he said. "You mean, this is Ontolo's invention?"

Bengati was still translating to the chief. The chief got Dr. Cooper's question and answered it through Bengati. "Like I said, Ontolo likes to make funny marks. He thinks he can make a piece of skin or bark speak words."

"He can!" Jay exclaimed.

"He is pretending," said the chief. "It is a game."

Jay received the skin back from his father and handed it to Ontolo. Then he bowed slightly and addressed the chief with proper respect. "If it please you, sir: Your son Ontolo has put *my* words on this skin, words he does not know but has still captured for all time." He turned to Ontolo. "Ontolo, go ahead: Read."

Ontolo was grinning, excited, and a little nervous as he began to speak the sounds his marks represented. "Een tah bee geening goad kree ate ted ta hay vons ond ta ert."

He looked up. His father seemed puzzled. Obviously the sounds were meaningless to him.

Dr. Cooper was more than pleased. He was awestruck. So was Dr. Henderson, and Lila.

"Is there more?" Dr. Cooper asked.

Jay nodded to Ontolo and Ontolo read some more. "Ond goad sayd late tare bee lite ond tare was lite."

Jacob Cooper chuckled, slowly shaking his head with wonder. "I see your point, Jay. This *is* history."

The chief noticed the response his son was getting from his visitors and asked Bengati about it.

Bengati was a bit awestruck himself and tried to explain.

Lila understood every word Ontolo had read, and repeated them all. "In the beginning, God created the heavens and the earth. And God said, let there be light, and there was light."

"Does Ontolo understand what he has read?" Dr. Cooper asked.

Bengati inquired of the boy, and then answered, "No. Ontolo doesn't know what he has read. He only knows the sounds your son Jay gave him to write down."

"This young man has invented a phonetic alphabet!" Dr. Henderson exclaimed.

"Bengati," said Dr. Cooper, "did *you* understand the words Ontolo just read?"

Bengati's eyes were wide with wonder as he answered, "At first, I did not. But then, when I heard more, I could tell: Ontolo was reading *your* words. English words."

"Tell Chief Gotono that his son has created a way to capture words—anyone's words—and place them on bark or stone or paper." Bengati started to explain this to the chief even as Dr. Cooper continued. "Because of this, your words, the words of your children, the stories of your ancestors . . . anything spoken, can be kept safe, for all time, for all generations."

The chief thought that over, then shrugged a little. He responded through Bengati, "The words of our mouths are kept safely in our heads. We remember the stories; we remember our ancestors and their names and what they did. We tell our children, and they tell their children."

Dr. Cooper respectfully countered, "But now you can receive and understand the words of other men as well. The pages of books can carry their words to you from far away." As Dr. Cooper said this, he opened his hands in front of him, pantomiming opening a book.

All motion in the room ceased abruptly. Chief

Gotono and Bengati stared at Dr. Cooper with widened eyes, then looked at each other. The sudden silence scared Jay and Lila. Had they caused a terrible offense somehow?

Bengati was the first to move again as he pressed his palms together in front of him. He opened them up as if opening a book, his eyes upon the chief, his lips quietly speaking words in Motosa.

The chief looked at Bengati's open hands, then at his creative son, and his lip began to quiver.

Bengati made the book opening gesture again, his eyes wide with wonder as he looked from his hands to Dr. Cooper and back again.

Finally, the chief opened his hands like a book, raised them toward heaven, and then, with deep, quaking sobs, he began to weep.

EIGHT

Back at Jo-Jota's, Dr. Henderson took a nap while the Coopers visited quietly on the porch, trying to figure out why the chief had suddenly dismissed everyone from his house. Chief Gotono had seemed so troubled, like he needed to be alone with his thoughts. The unveiling of Ontolo's phonetic alphabet had been a special moment, of course. But it seemed to have been the opening-a-book hand gesture that had made the chief weep, and he certainly had not attempted to explain why.

Their little meeting didn't last long. The village drummers, three men and an apprentice no older than ten, took their places outside the big meeting hall and began beating out an intricate, rhythmic song on deep, bass drums, a hollow log, and what appeared to be the steel wheel of an old car.

"It is time!" came a call from across the square. It was Bengati, coming on the run. "Come! We gather for our meeting!"

Lila wasn't ready for socializing. "Right *now?*"

Bengati beckoned. "Come. The chief will speak."

The Coopers scrambled to prepare. Jay didn't

have his shoes on, Dr. Cooper had to put on his shirt, and Lila needed to brush out her hair before she put on the headdress she'd made. As for Dr. Henderson, she didn't feel like going anywhere and started griping about it—whining, actually. But then her four loyal carriers showed up with her chair, and that settled that.

They hurried with the other villagers to the meeting hall and got there just in time. Bengati showed them to a log bench off to the side where he could quietly interpret the proceedings for them.

All the people, young and old alike, had gathered once again, sitting row upon row, dressed in colorful woven garments and dangling, clinking jewelry of leather, bone, and stone. There was a dull murmur in the crowd as people visited quietly; one or two babies cried.

Suddenly, without introduction or explanation, a man stepped onto the large, flat speaker's stone and started singing—or was it chanting? His voice was a powerful tenor, and the melody soared like the flight of a barn swallow. He sang a line of the song, and the people, as one voice, echoed it back with great power and hauntingly beautiful harmony. It gave Jay and Lila goosebumps.

The chanter delivered the next line of the song. The people echoed it back once again. Then came another line and another echo, and so it went. As the song progressed, it built in emotion and volume. As it ended, many in the group closed their eyes as if in prayer, closing themselves in with their own thoughts and feelings, their bodies swaying with the music.

More songs followed, and it was easy to see that these people weren't just having a singalong around a campfire. They meant deep, spiritual business.

Dr. Cooper was totally fascinated, leaning forward in his seat, watching and listening. Finally, he turned to Jay and Lila and said, "I think we're in church."

Jay and Lila nodded. That's what it looked, sounded, and felt like, all right. They stole a look at Dr. Henderson, and were startled to find that she was quite captivated, unconsciously swaying to the music, a rare smile on her face.

When the singing ended, it left a very sweet and peaceful mood about the place.

"Now the chief will speak," Bengati whispered.

With his full headdress in place and his arms outstretched, Chief Gotono got the immediate, respectful attention of his people. He began his speech—or was it a sermon?—in his characteristic, booming voice.

Bengati leaned close to the Coopers and Dr. Henderson and began to explain in a hushed voice what the chief was talking about. "The chief is telling the story of his father's father, Chief Landzi, who first brought our people here from across the desert and found water when he struck the rock."

When Bengati leaned away to listen some more, Dr. Cooper exchanged a quizzical, puzzled look with his kids.

"Dad," said Jay, "doesn't this sound like the story of Moses?"

Dr. Cooper had no time to answer. Bengati was

leaning toward them again, quietly recounting the chief's message out of the corner of his mouth. "Now the water is gone, but the chief says that if we turn from evil and seek after God, God will answer us and bring us water from the mighty Stone in the desert."

The chief raised his voice even louder and pointed west toward the mountain-sized Stone. Bengati explained, "The chief says that God has sent His holy mountain to speak to the tribe. Just as He sent Ontolo to save Mobutu, He has sent this Stone."

"Ontolo? Are you talking about—" Jay started to ask, but the sermon ended and another song began. This time the people stood to sing, clapping and waving their hands.

When the meeting ended, Dr. Cooper suggested, "Let's get back to Jo-Jota's and compare notes. The whole idea of the Motosas being savages and cannibals just doesn't hold up."

They sat on the big front porch and watched the village kids play while Jo-Jota brought them slices of bread and melon to snack on.

Dr. Henderson took a refreshing bite of melon and commented, "Sure, I found their rituals fascinating and their music enjoyable, but I see nothing unusual about their religious beliefs. They believe they've offended their god and so their god has taken away their water. It seems an appropriate myth for a primitive, agricultural society."

"That's not what's unusual," said Dr. Cooper, "What's unusual is that their religious system has no trappings of paganism: no magic rituals, no appeasing of evil spirits, no nature worship . . ."

"No idols," Lila added.

"That's right," said Jay. "And they only have one god, not several."

"That's the first thing that caught my attention," said Dr. Cooper, leaning forward in his chair. "They don't have a rain god, or a sun god, or a god of fertility, or a god of the crops or seasons or whatever. Their god is bigger than all that. Consider that Stone out there. Any other pagan culture would have fallen into worshiping that thing, sacrificing to it, chanting and using magic to appease it. But these people have a god big enough to have created it and put it there. Their god is bigger than nature, bigger than creation."

Dr. Henderson finished chewing her piece of melon. "Dr. Cooper, I suppose you want to believe that these people are Christians or something?"

Jay, Lila, and Dr. Cooper all checked each other's eyes and knew immediately that they shared the same suspicion. Dr. Cooper put it into words. "They may not be Christians in the way we would think— not Baptists, or Methodists, or Pentecostals. But considering that no modern-day missionary has ever come to these people to preach Christianity, I can't help wondering about the similarities."

"What similarities, if I may ask?" said Dr. Henderson.

"One god, bigger than all creation, who created all things, who tells these people what is right and wrong."

Jay piped in, "He teaches them that stealing is wrong, that they should work hard and share."

"And it's obvious that these people have a personal relationship with their god. They love him."

Jay asked, "So who's the Ontolo the chief talked about? I mean, I don't think he meant his son when he spoke about how God sent Ontolo to save Mobutu."

"And who is Mobutu," Dr. Cooper asked, "other than our somewhat shady host on the other side?"

Jay had already decided, "I'm going to ask Ontolo. I want to hear that story."

Dr. Cooper nodded. "And I'm going to have a heart-to-heart talk with the chief to find out where their religion really came from, where they got their stories and traditions."

"Like the one about the snake," said Lila.

They looked at her curiously.

"Don't you remember? When Renyata thought Ontolo had stolen Jay's pencil, she said that Ontolo was bitten by the snake, and that's why he did wrong."

Jay's and Dr. Cooper's faces brightened with recollection.

And then, like a bolt of electricity, the possible meaning of that expression hit them all.

"Ooohhhh boy . . ." said Lila.

"Where's Bengati?" Dr. Cooper asked, jumping to his feet.

The chief agreed to meet with Jacob Cooper the next morning. When Dr. Cooper arrived, the chief was sitting outside behind his home, carefully carving another staff, this one for his son.

"The staff of my father tells the story of our family in pictures," he said through Bengati. "But now I think Ontolo will want a staff on which he can make his own marks."

Dr. Cooper and Bengati sat with Chief Gotono under the shade of the big tree his house was built around. It was just the three of them, and the chief seemed quite relaxed. Dr. Cooper hoped this would be a good time to ask some big questions. Through Bengati, they began to converse.

"Chief Gotono, I hope all is well."

"All is very well, Dr. Cooper. I have had much to think about in a short time. You are right. Ontolo's strange marks can capture words that will remain for all time and can bring us the words of other men. Our God has chosen many ways to speak to us, but I never thought He would speak through the little marks created by my own son."

"Chief Gotono, can you tell me how you came to know your god?"

The chief looked thoughtfully at the staff he was carving as he spoke and Bengati translated. "There was once a young man who had many gods. His gods were in the sun, and in the moon, and in the trees, and in the crops. Some gods helped his people bear children, and some gods took the children away through death. But there were too many gods, and they were too small, and they would not speak. They would not tell the people what is right and what is wrong.

"So, this young man knew in his heart that there

had to be one God who made all things and supplies all things and can teach the people how they should live."

The chief looked toward the rugged mountains that rose above the grassy plain, his thoughts going back into history. "I journeyed into the desert and knelt in the sand, asking this great God to reveal Himself. And God spoke to me and said, 'Because you seek me with all your heart, you will learn of me, for I will reveal myself in everyday things.' And so it has been." The chief smiled, but his eyes were still sad. "We have heard from our God, but we still wait to hear His name, to know who He really is."

Dr. Cooper's heart went out to this man. "Chief Gotono, there is a wonderful book you must see." He pressed his palms together, then opened them as if opening a book. He could tell the chief recognized the gesture immediately. "It will tell you the name of your God."

The chief held up his hand. "First, I must tell you a dream I had. But you must tell no one else."

Dr. Cooper agreed and listened to the dream.

Lila and Beset sat together in the grass in front of the chief's house, working on a headdress even more lovely than the first.

"Beset . . ."

"Yes, Lila?"

"Do you remember when your mother thought Ontolo had stolen the pencil from Jay?"

Beset cocked her head and focused on Lila with

her huge, dark brown eyes. "Yes. What is in your thinking?"

"Your mother said Ontolo was bitten by the snake. What does that mean?"

Beset smiled, removed the headdress from Lila's head, and then spoke as she adjusted its size. "It means, Ontolo has done a bad thing. Ontolo did not steal pencil, but my mother did not know, so she say Ontolo bitten by the snake." She looked at Lila directly. "You are good. Your father, your brother, they good. But many people are bad. They do bad things, they are not kind. We say they are bitten by the snake. It is a story we tell."

Beset put the headdress on Lila's head again to check the size. "Long ago, we all had the same mother. You, me, my mother and father, all had the same mother. One day, a snake say to her, 'Come to my tree, and I give you something to eat,' but she say, 'I cannot eat your food, it will kill me.' But the snake say, 'No, you eat my food, you be very wise, and you never die.' So she come to the tree to get food, but then the snake bit her. He poison her. He put in her bad things: hate, and stealing, and bad thoughts and anger. And then she die."

She removed the headdress, satisfied with its fit, and picked up more yarn to weave around the headband. "Now all her children have the same poison. They do bad things, think bad things, and they die. So when someone do something bad, we say, 'They are bitten by the snake.'"

Lila could feel her heart pounding and her hands shaking. She tried to relax, not wanting Beset to be concerned, but her voice still quivered just a bit when she asked, "Beset, where did that story come from?"

Beset shrugged. "It is a story we tell. And now Ontolo has made the story on skins with his little marks."

"We have a story like that. It's—"

"Dad!" came a cry from the forest beyond the village. It was Jay's voice, and he sounded absolutely beside himself. "Dad! Lila!"

Lila and Beset leaped to their feet, expecting something terrible, and ran to the edge of the forest. Dr. Cooper and Chief Gotono had heard Jay's cry and also came on the run.

"Dad!" came Jay's voice again.

"Jay!" Dr. Cooper responded. "Where are you?"

They heard the thrashing of brush and the pounding of footsteps and finally saw Jay and Ontolo racing out of the forest like two wild men.

Jay spotted his father and dashed over, grabbing him. "Dad! You won't believe it!"

Dr. Cooper suddenly had his hands full of wildly excited son. "Are you all right?"

"You won't believe it!" Jay hollered again. "Back there, in the forest!"

"What!? Jay, calm down!"

"Ontolo showed me, he told me about it, and you'll never believe it!"

The chief was grilling Ontolo, trying to find out what all the hubbub was about. Ontolo wasn't nearly as excited, but he was getting a real kick out of watching Jay have a fit. He started to give his father an explanation.

"You gotta see it, Dad!" Jay insisted, tugging at his father. "You won't believe it!"

Dr. Cooper had to get firm. "Won't believe *what?*"

Jay finally got it out. "The Man in the Tree!"

Dr. Cooper immediately looked at the chief, hoping for some explanation.

By now the chief had been brought up to date by his son, and he answered, "Ontolo!"

Dr. Cooper didn't know what to think of that and just stood there, waiting to hear more.

Jay was giddy with excitement. "Ontolo! The name Ontolo means Man in the Tree! I thought it meant Man of the Woods or something, but it means Man in the Tree!" He tugged his father's arm again. "Come on! You won't believe it."

Lila was one big bundle of curiosity. "Let's go!"

"Where are we going?" Dr. Cooper asked as he followed his son.

"Ontolo!" the chief said again with a laugh. "Man in the Tree!"

Dr. Cooper looked around for Bengati and found him, following right behind. "I am here, Dr. Cooper. Don't worry."

They entered the forest, walking down a well-beaten path among the giant, gnarled trees that had stood here for centuries through rain, drought, wind, and sun.

Dr. Cooper asked Bengati, "What is it we're going to see?"

Bengati looked at the chief, who began to relate a story as Bengati translated. "There once was a young man who stole a pig from a neighboring tribe. When warriors from that tribe tried to chase him, he came to this forest and hid in a tree. They would have found him, except a bolt of lightning struck a tree nearby, breaking off a large branch and leaving a scar on the tree that was shaped like a man. The warriors saw that shape, and shot their arrows at it. They thought they had killed the thief, and so they left."

This sounded like the chief's other story about the young man, Dr. Cooper thought. "And you were that young man, Chief Gotono?"

The chief smiled and came to a stop by a huge tree with deeply furrowed bark and thick limbs. With a wide sweep of his hand, he indicated the trail that still wound through the forest toward the mountains. "I was the young man who fled with a stolen pig. I ran up this very trail," he pointed to the huge tree beside him, "and climbed this very tree. There is the branch on which I sat while my pursuers came looking for me."

Now the chief grew very solemn, his hard gaze commanding everyone's attention. "But do you understand, Dr. Cooper, that our God saved me from my pursuers when I deserved to die? God sent lightning from the sky and put another man in a tree to take my punishment."

The chief turned onto a side trail that led through the brush toward another tree as large and gnarled as the first. The others followed. He stopped on the far side of the tree and looked up, pointing. "Ever since that night, our people have remembered the Man in the Tree who took away my punishment, and I have given his name to my son as a remembrance."

Jay and Lila got to the front of the tree before their father. Dr. Cooper could see Jay pointing and Lila looking, and then he saw Lila's face go pale as her eyes widened with awe—or was it fear?

He came around the tree and looked up to see where the chief was pointing.

And then he froze as well. Words failed him. All he could do was look and try to believe what he was seeing.

About twenty feet up the big, gnarled trunk, a large limb had been blasted off by lightning, leaving a gaping scar where wood and bark had been torn away. The shape of the scar looked like a man: Bark had been peeled to form a body and two legs, and where two upper limbs had broken off, the scars looked like the man's outstretched arms. Just above the arms, a burl formed the shape of a drooping head.

The Man in the Tree appeared to be impaled there, hanging by his arms. A few broken arrows could still be seen embedded in the bare wood, shot there by the chief's pursuers so long ago, and part of a spear was still embedded in the man's side.

NINE

The Man in the Tree . . ." Jay said in a hushed voice. "On-To-Lo."

Dr. Cooper quoted the chief's words as a question, "'God sent Ontolo to save Mobutu'?"

Bengati asked the chief about it, and the chief nodded and answered through Bengati, "Mobutu was my name when I was young, before I became Gotono, the chief. That night, God showed me my guilt and the price that guilt can bring, but He paid the price Himself and let me live to do what is right. He spoke to me and revealed Himself, just as He said He would. I returned the pig to its owners and also gave them two of my goats to pay for my wrong. I have never stolen again, and my people have learned never to steal. Through Ontolo, the Man in the Tree, our God has spoken."

"Just like the Lady and the Snake," said Lila, tugging on her father's arm.

"What's that?" Dr. Cooper asked.

"Beset just told me another story. Listen to this." She quickly recounted it to her father and brother.

They were awestruck, overwhelmed.

"Man, oh man, oh man," Jay muttered.

"Your God *has* spoken," Dr. Cooper told the chief in a hushed voice. "I must tell you, we have stories just like yours of a lady and a snake and especially of a man nailed to a tree—" Suddenly his legs felt weak and shaky.

Lila's legs seemed to be trembling as well, and she almost lost her balance.

Jay looked down to see if he'd stepped on uneven ground.

Then a low, ominous, rumbling sound reached their ears. The branches of the big trees began to quiver overhead; the leaves began to tremble.

The chief shouted a phrase as he toppled to his knees, his eyes skyward. Bengati toppled as well as he translated, "He speaks again! Our God speaks again!"

"The Stone!" Dr. Cooper exclaimed.

They started to run back up the trail, staggering, weaving to and fro, bracing themselves against one tree and then another as the ground constantly shifted under their feet. They could not see the Stone from these woods, but they could still hear the deep, rumbling sound, like a mighty avalanche, echoing all around them.

When they finally emerged from the trees, they met Dr. Henderson, hopping and hobbling toward them, using a long stick for a crutch and fighting every second to remain on her feet. "Dr. Cooper, where have you been? The Stone's waking up!"

The earth reeled again. Jacob Cooper ran to Dr. Henderson and caught her just before she fell. "Hang onto my arm."

She grabbed on, dropping the stick. Together they

hurried up the path as the ground continued to rumble under their feet. Motosas ran from their homes, down the paths, and through their village.

But wait. The villagers were not running in panic or fear. They were hurrying—men, women, and children—out of the village and onto the open grasslands where they gathered like excited spectators to gawk at the Stone, pointing, chattering, even praying. To see the looks on their faces, this wasn't a dangerous natural event—it was a spiritual visitation!

"We've got to get out there," Dr. Henderson gasped, trying to walk. "We've got to observe what it's doing."

The rumbling began to subside; the shaking settled down to a small quiver. By the time they reached the village square, the earth was quiet again. The village was empty, but nothing appeared to be damaged, and apparently no one was hurt.

"We need the binoculars and the surveying equipment," said Dr. Henderson. "We have to note *any* changes in size, shape, position—*anything.*"

"I'll get my knapsack!" said Lila, running back toward Jo-Jota's.

"We'll have to bring the transit from the airplane," said Dr. Cooper.

"Let's get out there!" said Dr. Henderson.

The Motosas were starting to trickle back into the village. For now the show was over.

"Good thing the villagers are coming back," said Dr. Henderson. "That thing's unstable. It could erupt; it could topple; pieces of it could break off . . . . We don't know *what* it could do."

"We're going out to study it," Dr. Cooper told the chief. "But please, tell your people to remain here. It may not be safe to get too close."

The chief nodded and gave the order. The Motosas called to their stragglers, who began to return. Then Chief Gotono said to Dr. Cooper in English, "But I will come. I will see Stone, hear Stone speak."

Lila returned with her knapsack. "Here's the equipment. Did I miss anything?"

"Not yet," said her father, taking the knapsack. "But I think I see a problem developing." He noticed the look on Ontolo's and Beset's faces when they saw Jay and Lila all set for a trek into the desert.

Ontolo started to argue with his father, pointing at Jay and Lila, and it was easy to guess what the topic was.

"Uh, Jay and Lila," said Dr. Cooper, "I have a difficult favor to ask of you, and I hope you'll understand. You know I'd take you along without hesitation, but you see the situation developing here? If you go with us, then Ontolo and Beset will want to go, and if they can go, then the rest of the villagers will feel they should be able to go as well, and we'll end up creating a huge safety risk."

Both Jay and Lila slouched with disappointment. They couldn't help it.

"Guess you're right," Lila moaned.

Jay needed a moment to think it over but then called to Ontolo, "Ontolo! Let's go! Show me your game!"

That sounded good to Ontolo. With Jay and Lila in the lead, the four kids ran back into the village.

Dr. Henderson was impressed. "Those are good kids you have."

Dr. Cooper nodded as he watched them go. "The best." He started picking up the equipment. "Shall we?"

Ontolo ran home and returned to the village square with a weird, fuzzy ball fashioned from goathide and stuffed with nutshells instead of being inflated with air. All he had to do was walk through the square with that thing and all the other children came running, ready to break into teams and get the game going. Lila was assigned to Ontolo's team; Jay was assigned to the other team, captained by a friend of Ontolo named Suti.

Beset, knowing the most English, explained the rules to Jay and Lila, pacing off the boundaries of the playing field in the village square. "Jay kick ball this way . . . Lila kick ball *this* way . . ." The game looked like a combination of soccer and basketball: the ball was moved with the feet, but tossed by hand through a squarish goal once the player was close enough.

Ontolo's team threw the ball into play from the sidelines and the game began. Jay and Lila had both played soccer as well as basketball, so they were able to dive right into the game and keep the ball moving. The Motosa kids didn't know English, but they knew a good game when they saw it. Before long, Jay and Lila were fully accepted as valuable teammates, and when Jay scored his first point, his teammates were ready to make him an honorary Motosa.

At the edge of the grasslands, on the brink of the desert, Dr. Henderson and Dr. Cooper could see things were stirring around the Stone. A thin cloud of dust still lingered above the desert floor from the quaking, and high above the Stone's crest, ice particles that had been shaken loose were being carried away in wispy clouds by the wind.

Dr. Henderson scanned the upper edge through binoculars. "I don't want to believe this, but we might have some expansion happening along the top edge."

She handed Dr. Cooper the binoculars, and he checked it out. Almost two miles above them, the sharp edge of the Stone had a white, frosty edge. Large cracks had appeared in the ice as if the edge had stretched. "I see what you mean." Then he gave the binoculars back and directed her attention to the Stone's northwest corner. "And unless my eyes deceive me, there's a new ridge of dirt piled against the Stone."

She could see freshly disturbed earth all along the Stone's length, just like dirt pushed in front of a bulldozer's blade. "My *word!* It's growing. And yet . . . there are no growth cracks in the Stone itself, only in the ice and in the earth at the base."

She handed the binoculars to Chief Gotono and Bengati, who called them the Big Eyes. Having heard Dr. Cooper and Dr. Henderson's conversation,

Bengati was able to explain to the chief what was happening, and the chief nodded as he saw it for himself.

"We'll get the transit from the airplane to do some sightings," said Dr. Cooper. "Let's pace things off and triangulate and see if what we think has happened has really happened." With help from the chief and Bengati, Dr Cooper and Dr. Henderson began to measure the Stone's new dimensions.

At that very moment, high atop the rocky cliffs that pressed against the Stone's north end, three figures stole carefully over the rocks until they found a hiding place in a deep crack. They were tough, battle-hardened scouts from Idi Nkromo's army, dressed in camouflage fatigues and armed with rifles, pistols, and knives. They had hiked, climbed, and explored these hills for a day and a night, trying to find a route over them and around the Stone. Their efforts were finally rewarded. From this vantage point, they could view the entire desert on the Stone's west side, and through binoculars they spotted Dr. Cooper and Dr. Henderson, along with two men from the Motosa village—just four tiny figures on the barren landscape. They muttered words of victory to each other and started to lay plans.

Dr. Cooper scribbled some calculations on his writing pad, gazed through the transit one more time to doublecheck, and then ran the numbers again. "Well, the figures confirm what we've seen: The Stone has grown roughly 240 feet in both height and width."

"And yet it hasn't changed shape at all," Dr. Henderson mused. Dr. Cooper looked long and hard at the Stone, coming to a conclusion he found difficult. "The Stone isn't real, is it—not in the normal, material sense?"

Dr. Henderson thought the question over, then shook her head. "It's there, it's observable, and by all appearances it's physical. It's as hard as a diamond, maybe harder. It's shaking and gouging the earth. And yet, you're absolutely right: There *is* something unreal about it." She looked at him, and he could see fear in her eyes. "I guess I'm trying to say it's not of this world."

The village square had never seen such a hubbub. The two white-skinned foreigners turned out to be fierce competitors, very good with their feet, and their skill and determination only made the others play harder, loving every minute of it. The grown-ups, fascinated and amused by the sight, began gathering on the porches and along the edges of the playing area to cheer their teams on. Beset had scored a goal for Suti's team, but Lila came right back by catching a rebound off a teammate's head and hurling the ball through the goal. The score was even, three to three.

Suti took the ball out of bounds for his team as

arms went up everywhere trying to block his throw. Jay scurried into the clear along the side boundary line, and Suti shot the ball to him.

Blocked! A tall, stringbean of a kid diverted the ball with his hand, and it went sailing toward one of the houses. Lila was closest and went racing after it, hoping to take possession before it went out of bounds.

Too late. The ball rolled over the line, bounced through a flock of chickens that went scurrying and flapping, then rolled under a house. Lila dropped to her hands and knees, brushed the grass aside, and peered into the dark recesses under the thatched structure. She thought she saw the ball resting near a large corner post that held the house up, so she hurried closer on her hands and knees. Yes, there was the ball, almost hidden behind the large square stone that served as a footing for the post.

She reached for the ball. It was just beyond the reach of her fingertips. She stretched further—then stopped.

The kids were eager to continue the game. She could hear them shuffling and waiting.

But for the moment, her mind and eyes were pulled away from the lost ball. She turned her head and took a second look.

A large, square, reddish stone . . .

Now the kids were hollering at her. She could hear Beset calling, "Hurry up! Hurry up!"

She brushed aside some grass with her hand. The stone was cut, chipped, chiseled into a square shape. It was—

So suddenly it startled her, a ray of sunlight broke through the grass and shadows and lit up the side of the footing stone, making it sparkle. She spun her head and looked toward the east.

Just over the tops of the houses, through the leafy treetops, she saw the sun peeking over the top of the Stone in the desert like a fiery sunrise. One thin beam of light pierced through the trees, seeking out that one little stone right next to her.

"Jay," she called, her voice choked with fear, excitement, awe, shock, amazement. She called again, "Jay!" and then she nearly screamed, "JAY!"

He came on the run, afraid she'd hurt herself, been bitten by a snake or spider, broken a leg, gotten pinned under the house. "What! Are you all right?"

"Jay . . ." By now she was panting with excitement, rising to her knees, pointing at the foundation stone. "Jay, look!"

Jay looked and saw the foundation stone. He didn't get her point.

And then he did. He cocked his head to one side and looked again, his eyes tracing the beam of light from the little foundation stone to the sun now rising over the Stone in the desert. Pieces, thoughts, ideas were coming together in his mind.

Lila had already put several things together. "It's a foundation stone, Jay! It holds the house up!"

By now, Ontolo and Beset had come over to see what all the fuss was about. "Lila is hurt?" Beset asked.

Lila didn't answer that question but quickly

asked them a question of her own. "Do *all* the houses have stones like this?"

Ontolo looked at Beset who translated the question as best she could, but neither of them seemed sure they'd understood Lila correctly.

Lila scrambled to see for herself. She ran around to the rear corner of the house, swished the grass aside, and found another reddish, square stone just like the first. Jay went with her, and soon they discovered that not only this house, but also just about every house, was sitting on the same, reddish, square stones.

"Ontolo," said Jay, his voice broken with excitement. "Ontolo, why?"

Ontolo's face said, *Why what?*

"Beset." Jay beckoned to her urgently. "Beset, why are the houses built on these stones?"

She understood the question, but shrugged as if it held no importance. "Houses . . . stay strong. Houses not sink."

Lila and Jay exchanged excited looks.

"I think I'd better go and get Dad," Lila said with a trembling voice.

Jay concurred. "I think you're right."

Lila took off running through the village square, out of the village and out over the grasslands.

But no sooner had she left when there was a rustling and babbling in the crowd and Jay looked up to see the chief and Bengati returning from another direction, along with Dr. Cooper and Dr. Henderson.

"Dad!" he called.

Dr. Cooper and the other three could tell something was brewing. The chief asked immediately, "What happen here?"

114

Jay beckoned to them and then pointed to the foundation stone Lila had uncovered. "Bengati, why are all the houses built on these stones?"

Both the chief and Bengati chuckled as if they'd heard a silly question. Bengati answered, "To keep the houses from sinking into the ground. Long ago, it rained much, and then the ground would become soft and the houses would sink and the posts would rot. So we learned to build upon these stones."

"But . . ." Jay wasn't getting the answer he wanted. "But every house is built this way. Is this, you know, another tradition?"

Bengati was translating for the chief, who explained as Bengati interpreted, "Yes. It is something taught us by our forefathers. The rocks are like our God, you see? Our God is like a solid stone under our feet to keep us from sinking. When I stand on a large stone in our meeting hall, and when we build our houses this way, it shows us how we must build our lives upon our God."

Jay pointed at the foundation stone. "Why are they cut square?"

Bengati and the chief exchanged puzzled looks as if they'd heard another silly question, and then Bengati ventured an answer. "So they will not roll. So they will stand there and not move."

Dr. Cooper was already looking to the east as Jay said, "Look, Dad! Look at the Stone! It's cut out, carved, just like the foundation stones. It's square, and flat, and solid, and doesn't roll away."

Jacob Cooper was also figuring it out. "The wise man . . ." he murmured as he looked at the huge Stone in the desert and then at the small foundation stone. "Matthew chapter seven: 'Everyone who hears these things I say and obeys them is like a wise man. The wise man built his house on rock. It rained hard and the water rose. The winds blew and hit that house. But the house did not fall, because the house was built on rock.'"

Bengati translated the words to the chief, and he nodded. "Yes," he said through Bengati, "this is our tradition."

Dr. Cooper's voice was hushed with awe. "In a way, the Stone *is* speaking!"

TEN

The chief and Bengati drew near as Dr. Cooper removed his hat, nervously ran his fingers through his blond hair, and bored holes in the ground with his eyes. Jacob Cooper was thinking, formulating, riddle-solving, overwhelmed by the thoughts now streaming into his head.

"The Stone," he muttered, "a stone of stumbling, a rock of offense . . . signs in the wilderness . . ." Then he stiffened as if hit with a bullet—it was actually another thought that came to him with the *force* of a bullet. "Water from the rock! Water from the rock, *of course!*"

Dr. Cooper dug out his notebook and pen and started scribbling down his thoughts even as he spoke them, mostly to himself, but also to Dr. Henderson and Jay. "God spoke in special ways in the Bible; He used object lessons like . . ." Scribble scribble. "The tabernacle in the wilderness . . . the brass serpent Moses raised on the pole . . . the sacrificial lamb, and Abraham almost sacrificing his son Isaac . . . the Passover feast before the Hebrews left Egypt . . . Jonah in the belly of the fish for three days and three nights . . . the stone that brought forth water when Moses struck it!"

"I don't get it," said Dr. Henderson.

Dr. Cooper was getting excited. "These people have been seeking after God. Their chief went into the desert and asked God to reveal Himself, and now I'm convinced that God has answered that prayer. He's been showing Himself to these people."

"Exactly," said Jay.

"He's been speaking in symbols, stories, object lessons: the story about the Lady and the snake, the account of the tribal chief who brought his people here and struck a rock that brought forth water, the Man in the Tree, the stones they build their houses on, and now . . ." Dr. Cooper took several steps across the square and extended his hand toward the mountainous Stone that towered like a sentinel over the village. "The Stone in the Desert! The greatest, mightiest Stone of all! A stone of stumbling, a rock of offense . . ."

"What?" Dr. Henderson exclaimed. "Would you mind decoding all this for me?"

Jacob Cooper was becoming jubilant as more scriptures came to mind. "Remember Jesus quoting the Old Testament scripture about the stone the builders rejected becoming the cornerstone? Jesus was referring to Himself. He was calling Himself the cornerstone, the stone upon which we build our faith, our very lives!"

"But for those who don't believe," Jay recalled, "he'd be a stone of stumbling and a rock of offense. He'd only get people upset."

"Like His Excellency Nkromo and his bunch on the other side," Dr. Cooper said with a wink.

Bengati translated all of Jacob Cooper's words, and as the people all around the square heard them, they were spellbound. The kickball game was forgotten. The children and fathers and mothers and warriors and workers began to draw closer, wanting to hear more.

Now Dr. Cooper turned to the Motosas and said, "People, I believe you are right about the Stone. I believe your God sent it."

Dr. Henderson sniffed a little chuckle. "Well, that's what you should have told them all along."

"For *your* God is also *my* God."

That turned her head. "But hey, take it easy!"

Dr. Cooper continued to speak as Bengati translated. "Your God has spoken to you through stories and traditions," he said, "and through the Man in the Tree. Now He speaks through this mighty Stone that He has sent!" Dr. Cooper thought of another scripture. "In the Bible . . ." He thought he'd better explain what the Bible was. "Uh, God's words, written for all to see—"

The chief broke into a glowing smile and made the opening-a-book hand gesture. "My dream, Dr. Cooper. Remember my dream!"

That got Dr. Cooper all the more excited, to the point of preaching. "The words of God say that the stone is precious to those who believe, but will be hated and rejected by those who do not believe. Well, we were always wondering why you were never afraid of the Stone when the people who live in the east are terrified. Now we understand. No one has to be afraid of the Stone if they know the Savior it represents. Chief Gotono, we know this Savior! We know His name! He is—"

Just then, everyone heard a distant scream coming from the desert.

"What was that?" Dr. Henderson asked, alarmed.

Dr. Cooper knew his daughter's voice. "Lila!" He looked around immediately, verifying she was not present.

Jay suddenly came to awareness. "Oh man, in all the excitement I forgot! She went into the desert to look for you!"

"What?"

"She saw that stone under the house and made the connection and ran to get you to tell you and . . ."

"And she's still out there?"

Chief Gotono had heard the scream as well. "Lila, your girl?"

"Yes!"

The chief bellowed the information to his people, and there was an immediate babble of concern. Some of the kids were ready to run right out and find Lila but were held back by protective parents. Several warriors, better skilled for the task, ran for their spears.

"We go," said the chief. "We find the girl Lila!"

Dr. Henderson grabbed the stick she'd been using as a cane. "And I'm going too."

Dr. Cooper and Jay, Dr. Henderson, Chief Gotono, Bengati, and six warriors hurried out of the village and across the grasslands, calling Lila's name, fanning out, heading for the desert.

Chief Ontolo sent his warriors in several different directions, some south and north across the grasslands and some straight into the desert. Then he, Bengati, Dr. Cooper, and Jay ran straight ahead, toward the Stone, calling Lila's name. Dr. Henderson followed as quickly as she could.

They came to the place where Dr. Cooper and the others had set up the transit and done the surveying and calculations. It was the most likely spot where Lila would have come in her search for them, but she was nowhere to be found.

The chief shouted in a voice with the power of a ship's horn, "LILA!"

The Stone echoed back with incredible clarity, "LILA!"

They crossed the grasslands while warriors continued to search to the north and south of them, then pressed on into the desert where rocks the size of houses and cars cluttered the sandy landscape as if they'd fallen from the sky. The afternoon sun was growing hot, and the desert was becoming like an oven. They wouldn't last long out here without shelter—but neither would Lila.

They spread out, the chief to the right, Bengati to the left, the Coopers and Dr. Henderson straight ahead. The terrain was getting rougher, rockier. Dr. Cooper, Jay, and Dr. Henderson had to start climbing over and working their way around massive rock formations.

When they reached the bottom of a rocky hollow, Dr. Cooper stopped. "She wouldn't have come this way looking for us. She knew we were surveying, and you can't do that from here."

They started to turn back.

Three soldiers, rifles ready, leaped from behind the rocks and stood in their path. It happened so quickly it startled them, and Dr. Henderson almost lost her balance.

They heard a clattering on either side and saw more soldiers, at least twenty, popping up from behind the rocks, aiming rifles at them. They were surrounded, with no way to escape.

They raised their hands in surrender. The soldiers rushed in, shouting orders they couldn't understand, grabbing them, checking them for weapons, handling them roughly.

Dr. Cooper tried to explain their situation. "I'm Dr. Jacob Cooper and—"

An officer hauled back his arm as if to strike him.

Dr. Cooper shut his mouth and said no more.

Jabbing with their rifles, the soldiers forced them to walk, and they began the hazardous journey to the forbidding and treacherous hills that pressed against the Stone's north side.

The forced hike around the Stone and down into the desert to the east took several long, grueling hours. Prodded along by their captors, Dr. Cooper, Jay, and Dr. Henderson followed a twisting, winding, barely discernible path through the rock formations and boulders, up steep rock faces, over featureless, rocky shelves as hot as a griddle, and along narrow ledges with hardly enough room to walk. When Dr. Henderson lagged behind, the soldiers half-carried, half-dragged her to make her keep up.

Steadily, painfully, they made it out of the hills

and down to the flat desert on the Stone's east side, their feet and ankles aching, their bodies exhausted, their throats dry and crying out for water.

Then came a sight all three had expected. Up ahead, among the large, scattered rocks, the armies of Idi Nkromo had pitched camp in the shadow of the Stone. His Excellency must have developed new boldness to venture this close.

They entered the army camp past the camou-flaged, desert-colored tents where soldiers nervously cleaned their guns, sharpened their knives, and watched them pass with steely, cold expressions. All of Nkromo's trucks, tanks, and cannons were there, lined up in a row, facing west, as maintenance personnel swarmed over them quickly, frantically, like ants in a disturbed anthill. There was tension in the air, as tight as an overwound clock. And fear. The Coopers noticed how often the soldiers looked to the west to see what the Stone might be doing.

They reached the center of the camp and stood before an especially large tent. By all the colorful banners draped across its front, the rope fence stretched all around it, and the armed guards watching over it, they easily guessed that it was the field barracks of His Excellency, Field Marshal Idi Nkromo.

"Dad!" came a welcome voice.

Dr. Cooper's heart leaped as he saw Lila, safe, but in the custody of another band of soldiers. The soldiers released her to run to her father and brother, and she embraced them with tears in her eyes. "I went out to find you, and they grabbed me. I thought I'd never see you again!"

"It's okay, sis," said Jay. "We're together now, no matter what else happens!"

There was a shout and the beating of a huge drum. Any soldier not occupied with the prisoners snapped to attention and all eyes went toward the field marshal's tent. The tent door flapped open. Some guards stepped out to take their places on either side. Then, with as big and impressive an entrance as he could muster, His Excellency stepped out of his tent wearing battle fatigues, a kettle-sized helmet, a saber in a scabbard, and several pounds of medals. He was most unhappy and glared at the prisoners with big round eyes as he stomped toward them.

"Well . . ." said Jacob Cooper, spotting Chief Secretary D. M. Mobutu following right behind Nkromo, also decked out in fatigues, gold braids, and medals.

Nkromo stopped abruptly just a few yards in front of them, planting both feet in the sand with a precisely timed military stomp. D. M. Mobutu marched up smartly and stopped alongside his boss. Mobutu was looking a little shaky and seemed to be avoiding Dr. Cooper's eyes.

"So we meet again, Dr. Cooper!" Nkromo growled. "You and your band of thieves and traitors and spies! How dare you try to flee the country with my airplane!"

"What?" Dr. Henderson squawked. "That's the biggest pile of baloney I ever heard! We got caught in a storm and crashed! We almost got killed!"

Nkromo cocked an eyebrow. "You look fine to me."

Jennifer Henderson stuck out her injured leg. "Yeah, like I always walk around with a crutch!"

Dr. Cooper locked eyes with Mobutu. "Mr. Mobutu, you did tell him you provided us with that airplane, didn't you?"

Mr. Mobutu maintained a straight, military posture as he said, "If His Excellency says you stole the airplane, then you stole it."

Dr. Henderson had some choice words she wanted to share with Mobutu, but the president thundered, "You are traitors!" before anyone could say anything. "You were brought to this country to remove the Stone, and what do you do? You flee in a stolen government airplane and consort with the enemy!"

"The *enemy?*" Dr. Cooper reacted.

D. M. Mobutu stepped forward, looked to His Excellency to be sure he could speak, and then said, "You have consorted with His Excellency's enemies, the Motosas."

Jacob Cooper was horrified. "You can't be serious! The Motosas, your enemies? They mean no harm to anyone! You should be proud to have such good people as citizens of your nation!"

The two guards on either side of Nkromo raised their rifles threateningly. Mobutu held up his hand to call them off and then cautioned, "Dr. Cooper, please, remember whom you are addressing and guard your tone of voice."

Dr. Cooper calmed himself with great effort and spoke in a quiet, almost secretive tone. "Mr. Mobutu, just what is going on here?"

Mobutu shook his head with regret. "I warned you not to go into the land of the Motosas."

Jay retorted, "Yeah. You said they were cannibals and headhunters!"

Mobutu held up his hand to beg their patience. "I was hoping that would be enough to keep you away from them. I knew it would be certain death for you to be seen with those people."

Dr. Cooper guarded his tone as he explained, "Mr. Mobutu, really, we had no choice! We were caught in a storm and had to land!"

"That is not the way His Excellency sees it," said Mobutu. "His army scouts saw you consulting with Chief Gotono, and they saw your children playing a game with the Motosa children."

Dr. Cooper sighed. "We didn't know the Motosas were His Excellency's enemies. We saw no reason in the world why they should be." Then he added forcefully, "And we still don't!"

Mobutu kept trying to play the role of Chief Secretary of the Republic of Togwana, standing straight and sounding official. Even so, his hands were shaking, and when he spoke, the emotions he tried to hide gave his voice a little quiver. "His Excellency has done much to purge our nation of undesirables and rebel groups so that we may be one nation under Nkromo. The Motosas . . ." He had to swallow. "The Motosas have been declared undesirable and must be eliminated."

Lila gasped, incredulous. "No, you can't do that!"

Mobutu tried to explain. "The Motosas have a

special kind of faith which the, uh, Republic of Togwana cannot tolerate."

"Which *Nkromo* can't tolerate," Jay whispered to Lila.

Mobutu drew closer and lowered his voice as if speaking in confidence. "Only weeks ago, His Excellency was about to launch a war of extermination against them. He and his armies were prepared to slaughter them all, burn their village, and wipe their memory from the face of the earth."

"Until the Stone appeared," said Dr. Cooper.

Mobutu nodded. "It blocked his way, planted fear in his troops, thwarted his plans. He could not reach the Motosas. His cannons could not remove the Stone, and neither could his witch doctors. So we sent for you."

Dr. Cooper was insulted by the idea. "You wanted us to remove the Stone just so you could attack and kill a peaceful, virtuous people? You must be insane! Even if I could move the Stone, I would never—"

Mobutu shot up his hand in warning. "Do not say it, doctor. Your life hangs in the balance."

"You are spies!" Nkromo bellowed, pointing his big, fat finger at them. "You are siding with the enemy!"

Dr. Cooper took a fleeting moment to observe the tension in Nkromo's face, the nervous trembling in his hands. The tyrant was not as brave as he tried to appear. Dr. Cooper spoke clearly and carefully, choosing his words for their effect. "We have learned much about the Stone, if His Excellency is interested."

Nkromo gazed up at the Stone, trying not to look too interested. But he was very interested. "What have you learned?"

"We discovered it to be chiseled out, but not by human hands. The Stone is not of this world, Your Excellency." Dr. Cooper paused, considered, and then delivered the punch line. "We have concluded that the Stone can only be removed by the *God* who put it there."

"The God who—" Nkromo's eyes looked like they would pop, and he clenched his fists in rage. "You dare to speak to me of God? *Idi Nkromo* is god in Togwana!"

Dr. Henderson muttered to Dr. Cooper, "Your gift for diplomacy boggles the mind."

Nkromo took several steps toward Dr. Cooper and locked eyes with him. "God cannot stop Idi Nkromo! Idi Nkromo is not afraid!"

Dr. Cooper stood his ground, not flinching, not breaking his gaze with the ruthless tyrant, and finished his thought. "It is our conclusion, Your Excellency, that whoever challenges the Stone challenges *God!*" Dr. Cooper could see Mr. Mobutu out of the corner of his eye, and could tell his words were not being wasted on the Chief Secretary. Good.

As for Nkromo, he looked stunned for only a brief moment but then spoke defiantly, "We can go *around* the Stone! We will go *around* God!" Nkromo's eyes darted about, looking at all the soldiers watching him. "I sent soldiers to search, and they found a way, so we will go. The trucks and tanks and cannons cannot go, but my men can go."

He paused and looked around the parade ground. Dr. Cooper could tell Field Marshal Nkromo was performing for his troops, giving them a show of courage. "So it is the Motosas your God has hurt, not Idi Nkromo! Without the tanks and cannons, the Motosas will not die quickly." Nkromo was so amused by that thought his anger even subsided. He shouted more to his troops than to Dr. Cooper, "The Motosas will suffer before they die!"

The soldiers raised their rifles and cheered.

Mr. Mobutu cringed.

Dr. Cooper shot a glance at the Stone, now a towering silhouette in the afternoon sun, cold and silent—for now. "Mr. Nkromo, given the research data we have, I'm not sure God placed the Stone there just to block your path and protect the Motosas. He may have put it there to teach them—and you—a lesson."

"Your God will teach *me* nothing!" Nkromo snapped his fingers and the soldiers guarding them started shoving and yanking them along, moving them toward a large rock at the far end of the camp. "*I* will teach *you!* You are spies, and spies we shoot!" Nkromo waved his hand, and ten of his special guards came forward, rifles ready.

Lila, Jay, Dr. Cooper, and Dr. Henderson were shoved up against the big rock at gunpoint. The squad of ten soldiers lined up in a neat, straight line just thirty feet away, at attention, rifles at their sides, ready to hear the order to fire.

Nkromo came forward, ready to deliver that order, but first he drew a deep breath and pasted on a phony, gracious smile. "Dr. Cooper, I am merciful. I want you to live. Do you want to live?"

Jacob Cooper could hear some kind of deal coming and hesitated to answer.

Dr. Henderson spoke right up, even raising her hand. "Count me in!"

Nkromo extended his hands, palms up. "Then make the Stone go away, and I will know you are my friend! I will let you live." He shrugged. "Don't make it go away, and you will die."

Dr. Henderson sighed, her shoulders drooping.

Dr. Cooper remained resolute. "Your Excellency, I strongly advise you to listen to me. The power that lies behind the Stone is greater than any of us can begin to understand—"

"Ready . . ." Nkromo shouted. The ten riflemen raised their rifles, ready to shoot.

ELEVEN

Here's a fine mess you've gotten us into!" Dr. Henderson moaned.

Lila touched her brother's hand. "I love you, bro."

He looked back and smiled. "I love you, too, sis."

But then, a thought, a feeling, came to her. "Wait a minute." She crinkled her face as she considered it. "Something's going to happen!"

"Aim . . ." Nkromo yelled.

Dr. Cooper could see straight down the barrels of the ten rifles when he shouted, "Your Excellency! You hired us to study the Stone, and I have not finished giving you my report!"

The word *fire* was just on Nkromo's lips, but he didn't say it. He looked Dr. Cooper in the eyes, then raised his hand to hold back the riflemen. They relaxed, holding their rifles across their chests. Nkromo stepped forward impatiently. "What now?"

Dr. Cooper looked at the Stone, then back at Nkromo, with carefully timed, occasional glances at Mr. Mobutu. "You should know, the God who placed the Stone there is not just the God of the Motosas. He is the God of all men, to whom all men—even you, Mr. Nkromo—must bow, now or later. The Stone is a sign, a message from Him, and according to our written data . . ." Dr. Cooper drew a Bible passage from memory, "'The person who falls on this stone will be broken. But if the stone falls on him, he will be crushed.'" Nkromo started to smile in mockery, but Dr. Cooper wouldn't let him get away with that. "We took careful measurements, Mr. Nkromo! The Stone is growing, even as I speak! Based on the, uh, written data, there is a strong probability that the Stone will grow until it overruns you. It will strike you down, you and all your armies, and you will be swept away without a trace unless you humble yourself and honor the God who speaks through the Stone!"

Nkromo took that in and thought about it, his eyes glaring at Dr. Cooper and then at the Stone. His breathing was labored, his hands trembling. He was trying to look strong and unshaken, but Dr. Cooper could read the fear in his eyes. Finally, Nkromo spoke, his teeth clenched. "Dr. Cooper, I see nothing happening!"

"Well," Dr. Henderson tried to soothe him, "there *are* different interpretations of the data—"

"You will!" Dr. Cooper insisted.

Nkromo forced a smile. "When?"

Dr. Cooper looked heavenward for just a moment and then answered boldly, "Now!"

Nkromo backed away a step as if expecting something. All the soldiers were looking toward the

Stone with wide, frightened eyes. The ten men in the firing squad fell into disarray, muttering to each other, their rifles drooping toward the ground. Mr. Mobutu had his back against a big army truck, looking like *he* was about to be shot.

Dr. Henderson muttered, "Jacob Cooper, I almost hope you're right."

A long, suspenseful moment passed.

But nothing happened.

Nkromo broke into a smile, and then he laughed. Stepping quickly backward, he gave the order, "Ready!"

"Well, nice try," said Dr. Henderson.

"I still think something's going to happen!" said Lila.

The guards raised their rifles once again, though some of them seemed a little hesitant.

"Mr. Mobutu!" Dr. Cooper called. "You have known the God of the Motosas! You know the Stone is of God or you would not have sent for a godly man!" Mobutu was too timid to answer. "If you side with Nkromo now, you will perish with him!"

Mobutu just stood there, stiff with fright.

"Aim!" Nkromo shouted, his hand raised as a signal, and once again, the Coopers and Dr. Henderson were looking right down the long barrels. Nkromo was feeling cocky now. He kept his hand up, prolonging the moment. "Perhaps you would like to pray, Dr. Cooper—if you think God will hear you!"

Dr. Cooper sighed, then reached for Jay's hand as

Jay reached for Lila's. Then, surprisingly, Dr. Cooper felt Dr. Henderson grab his other hand. He looked her way, and she said simply, "Count me in."

He smiled and lifted his eyes toward heaven. A verse of Scripture came to mind, and he recited it. "'During danger he will keep me safe in his shelter. He will hide me in his Holy Tent . . . he will keep me safe on a high mountain.'"

Nkromo dropped his hand. *"FIRE!"*

Jay and Lila didn't remember hitting the ground. They only realized, suddenly, that they were lying in the sand, smarting a bit from the fall and wondering where the bullets had hit them. They could see their father, rolling in the sand and reaching for Dr. Henderson who was crying out, curled up in pain. The rifles had gone off; their ears were still ringing from all the shots.

But then they noticed something really odd: The soldiers in the firing squad were all on the ground too. Even Nkromo was rolling and wriggling in the sand, trying to get his feet under him again, having a fit, screaming at his soldiers.

And it wasn't just Nkromo and his firing squad; the whole army camp was on the ground, hollering, screaming, wriggling, and struggling to get up again.

Jay looked at Lila. "Something happened!"

She nodded back, starting to grin.

They struggled to their knees and checked themselves for wounds, but found none. The firing squad had missed. Everyone had been knocked down.

They were knocked down again as the earth gave another mighty lurch. Nkromo's men also toppled to the ground with a clattering of rifles and anguished cries of terror. The earth had come alive. It was shaking and rumbling, and the sound of thunder seemed to come from everywhere, pounding upward through the ground, throbbing in their ears, rattling the trucks and tanks and cannons and making the small rocks dance. The whole army camp was falling into chaos.

"Mr. Mobutu!" they heard their father shout. They could see him on his knees and one hand, pointing at Mobutu with the other hand. "Whom will you serve? Decide now!"

Mr. Mobutu was lying on his side, trying to prop himself up on one elbow, his eyes darting about as if witnessing the end of the world. His mouth was wide open as if to scream, but terror had stolen his voice.

Nkromo struggled to his feet and staggered about like a drunken man as the earth rolled and shifted under him, his long, silver saber in his hand. He waved his saber at the Coopers and Dr. Henderson and started screaming *"FIRE! FIRE!"* at his firing squad. The ten men regathered, grabbing onto each other for support as they struggled to their feet and got their rifles back in position to carry out his order.

"Mobutu!" Dr. Cooper yelled. "Choose!"

Mobutu finally got to his feet, his knees bent and his arms outstretched for balance as he beheld in horror the chaos around him.

"FIRE!" Nkromo screamed again, and once again the soldiers tried to aim their rifles toward the

Coopers and Dr. Henderson. In all the shaking and rumbling, the rifle barrels wavered and wiggled. The soldiers could hardly stand up.

"Mobutu!" Jacob Cooper yelled one more time.

From the west came a sound like an avalanche, like thunder, like a volcano erupting. It grew in intensity and shook the quaking ground even more.

Mobutu looked to the west, toward the Stone.

And then he decided.

He shouted something to the firing squad. Two of the soldiers looked his way. He gave them an order, and they immediately stepped out and trained their rifles on their fellow soldiers! The remaining eight looked at the two, then looked toward the Stone, and quickly reached a decision. They dropped their rifles and fled. The two soldiers closed in to protect the Coopers and Dr. Henderson, their rifles raised, preventing anyone from approaching them.

Jay and Lila got to their feet and staggered toward their father who was also standing and helping Dr. Henderson off the ground.

"Dad! Those two soldiers!" Lila shouted.

Dr. Cooper was smiling even as he held tightly to Dr. Henderson to help her balance. "I know. Bernard and Walter, Mobutu's two accomplices! I thought I recognized them."

Mobutu ran in a jerky, zigzag course and finally came near. "The God of the Motosas!" he yelled, pointing to the west. "You are right! He is bringing His destruction upon us!"

They all looked west and saw a sight their minds could not understand. The Stone looked higher than it ever had before, and now they could tell the top edge was slowly rocking like a monstrous ship on the ocean, heaving left, then right, growing, reaching, filling the sky with acres and acres of dark, stony expanse. All along the base of the Stone, a tidal wave of rock, dust, and sand was building higher and higher, rolling and tumbling toward them, dug up and pushed along by the sheer, flat face of the Stone.

"It's growing!" Dr. Henderson cried, shaking her head in utter astonishment. "Growing at a phenomenal rate!"

"Growing *and* moving," said Dr. Cooper. "It's headed this way."

Mobutu hollered to Bernard and Walter, who immediately ran away on an assignment. "They will bring a vehicle! We must flee for our lives!"

Nkromo's army had already decided on that course of action. Even though Nkromo was waving his saber and screaming for order and discipline, a thousand soldiers were looking to the west and seeing something bigger and far more frightening than Idi Nkromo.

They dropped their rifles—some even yanked off their boots so they could run faster—and started abandoning the camp, fleeing across the desert. Those closest to the trucks and tanks jumped inside and started them up as scores of soldiers swarmed onto the vehicles like flies on raw meat. With engines roaring and wheels and tracks spinning, the huge, green vehicles thundered through the camp, running over and through tents, smashing through tables and equipment, trampling anything that got in the way as they made their escape.

"Well let's not just *stand* here!" Dr. Henderson cried, pointing toward the Stone.

The Stone was picking up speed, closing on them faster and faster, moving over the desert like the very hand of God, scraping up a mountain of earth before it and rumbling like a million freight trains.

Bernard and Walter came running and staggering back with a bad report. Mobutu passed the news to the others: "There are no vehicles left! We'll have to flee on foot!"

Dr. Henderson yanked at Dr. Cooper's arm, trying to pull him east. "So come on, let's go!"

"No," said Dr. Cooper, looking at the advancing wall and the rolling, crashing wave of earth in front of it. "Not that way."

"*What!?*"

He pulled Jay and Lila close. "We'll run toward it. We'll run *toward* the Stone!"

"*Toward* the Stone?" Mobutu gasped.

Dr. Henderson could see the Stone still advancing, moving far faster than a human could run; she could also see the army fleeing, leaving clouds of dust behind their wheels, tracks, and feet and getting a very nice head start. "Cooper, you're crazy! You're out of your mind!"

"No, he's *right*," Jay countered. "Everything he's said about the Stone is coming true! The Stone *is* sent from God!"

"How can you believe that?" Dr. Henderson squawked.

"Just take a look," said Dr. Cooper.

She was already looking, of course. The desert floor was being ripped up and rolled up like a huge carpet before the Stone as it continued to advance. Large rock formations—some hundreds of feet high—were being smashed and disintegrated like glass bottles, the pulverized pieces flying hundreds of feet through the air, the sound of their destruction like exploding bombs.

"Even without that bad knee you couldn't outrun it," Dr. Cooper argued. "None of us could, and we certainly can't move fast enough to get around it."

"So we're dead . . ." she moaned.

"Not if . . ." Mobutu was still terrified, but beginning to see Dr. Cooper's point. "Not if God is merciful."

"He's merciful," said Dr. Cooper.

"Oh yeah, *right!*" said Dr. Henderson, watching the Stone demolish the desert.

Lila reached over and grabbed her arm. "Dr. Henderson, the Stone represents Jesus! If you really want to live, you don't run *from* Him; you run *to* Him!"

Dr. Henderson looked at Lila, then at the Stone, then at the retreating army still running, then at Dr. Cooper, and then she stood there, wrestling with the decision.

BOOM! Another rock formation the size of a skyscraper exploded into particles.

Dr. Henderson wilted, swayed her head, then finally spouted, "All right, all right!"

"That's the stuff!" said Dr. Cooper.

Bernard and Walter didn't even need an order from Mobutu. They just came up to Dr. Henderson, made a chair of their arms, and picked her up. Then the Coopers, Mr. Mobutu, Dr. Henderson, and Bernard and Walter set out across the desert, hiking directly toward the Stone without veering to the right or to the left.

It was tough going. The earth was still quivering and quaking under their feet, throwing them off balance, rocking them from side to side. All they could do was hold onto each other in a desperate effort to stay on their feet and keep taking one perilous, chancy step after another.

The desert terrain was no help. With the shaking, the sand often seemed to liquefy as it closed over the tops of their feet. They had to keep dodging around loose stones that rolled, danced, and tumbled over the ground like living things. The air was turning brown with dust that stung their faces and clogged their nostrils. They could feel the grit between their teeth.

OOF! A violent, sideways lurch knocked them all down and Dr. Henderson screamed in fear and pain. Bernard and Walter bore her up again, and they all kept going.

KARROOOM! A tall, teetering pillar of rock gave way and toppled like a big tree right in front of them. They leaped back, covering their heads as sand and pebbles rained down. Then, picking their way through the rubble, they kept going.

The top edge of the Stone blotted out half the sky and seemed to be splitting the whole world in half.

The rolling, tumbling mass of earth in front of the Stone had grown to the size of a small mountain range, and the roar of the cascading earth, sand, and stone was so loud it was the only sound anyone could hear.

Faith, Lila thought as she watched the mountain-sized pile of tumbling earth coming right toward them. *This has to be faith.*

"Lord," Dr. Cooper prayed, the thunder of the Stone's approach drowning out his voice, "receive us. Shelter us, I pray!"

"God," said Dr. Henderson, anticipating what it would feel like to have a cubic mile of earth come crashing down on top of her, "get us through this or take a gun and shoot me!"

All they could see was the Stone, the tumbling earth, the flying debris, the sky now brown with dust. They could feel the rush of dirty, dusty air being forced along ahead of the Stone's immense, flat surface.

The earth lurched again, and they toppled to the sandy ground. Looking up, they saw the Stone's top edge move across the sky directly overhead. They were being pummeled by small rocks and sand, the first particles of debris flying out from the mountain of earth the Stone was bulldozing before it.

This is it! Dr. Cooper thought. In only seconds they would be buried under a rolling mountain of debris.

They felt the ground stop shaking.

They looked all around. As far as they could see, the desert was quaking, shifting, shaking under a boiling shroud of dust.

But under their fallen bodies, the ground seemed perfectly solid, perfectly still. They looked at each other. *What's happening?* their eyes said.

Jay was the first to think his eyes were playing tricks on him. He blinked, looked several directions, then blinked again, trying to be sure he was really seeing the desert drop away all around them. "Hey . . ."

"Hang on," said Dr. Cooper. "Don't move!"

They all felt a sensation like going up in an elevator, and then their eyes confirmed that the brown, dusty mantle over the desert floor was dropping away. They were rising above it, just like an airplane flying up through the clouds into clear blue sky.

Lila's hand felt empty space. She looked, then screamed in horror and surprise and clutched at the earth that remained under her. Right next to where she lay was a sheer drop. Dirt and sand were still shifting and sliding over the edge. Dr. Cooper grabbed hold of her, and then they all grabbed each other as they realized the abrupt edge extended all around them.

They were resting on a platform, a weird-shaped chunk of desert floor that was rising higher and higher, and just in time. With a thunderous roar and a billowing cloud of dust, the massive pile of earth and torn up desert rolling in front of the Stone cascaded directly beneath them, tumbling and falling like a Niagara Falls made of earth. Strangely, they felt no quiver, no shaking, no danger. It was like standing on a safe look-out platform, high above it all.

Finally, they could see what had happened. A large arm of rock, an extension from the Stone, had risen up beneath them, lifting them and the desert floor they were lying on. Now it was drawing them in, shrinking in close to the sheer face of the Stone to form a wide, safe ledge. They could feel the wind rushing around them. The Stone was carrying them like passengers, cradling them on a safe ledge above the destruction as it continued to grow, slide, and tear up the desert.

Dr. Cooper was awestruck as he peered over the edge and watched the incredible cataclysm. "He will keep me safe in his shelter . . ." he said in wonder. "He will keep me safe on a high mountain."

Lila was squealing with delight. "I knew it! I knew God would take care of us!"

Jay was really enjoying the ride of his life. "Is this what you call the Rock of Ages?"

Dr. Henderson shook her head, totally bedazzled, shocked, awestruck. "You guys are too much!"

"Now do you believe?" Lila called over the noise.

Dr. Henderson peered over the sheer edge at the tumult below. They were riding—it seemed like flying—over the desert several hundred feet in the air, the wind rushing around them, the earth boiling, shaking, tumbling, and rumbling beneath them. It was like having a comfortable box seat from which to observe the end of the world—or its creation. "This is . . . this is unbelievable!" Then she added, "But I believe it!"

To the west of the Stone, across the wide grasslands, Chief Gotono and all the Motosas braced themselves against the old trees that sheltered their village and watched in holy amazement as the mountain from God moved. It was sliding, rumbling, digging its way away from them, moving toward the cities and people of the east. Beneath them, the ground quivered and rumbled, but it was nothing dangerous. Every Motosa, young and old, was accounted for and every home was solidly built on stone footings. The people would be all right; their houses would stand.

In awe, several Motosas fell to their knees and cried out to God for understanding. Many came to the chief and asked him the meaning of it all, but he only told them to keep watching, and to pray. Understanding would come later, he said. God was speaking again, and soon they would know His message.

But what was that new sound? A trickling, a babbling, and then a rushing . . . like a river.

The chief looked down at his feet just as water swirled around his toes. It was cool and brown from the silt it had picked up on its way across the grasslands, but it was water! He cried out, not in fear, but in boundless joy. Then he started shouting to the others, waving at them to come look.

They came on the run and watched the long, meandering ditch they had dug fill with rushing water!

They left the shelter of the trees and started running across the grasslands to see more of this miracle. When they came over a rise, they shouted, they screamed, they danced for joy and amazement.

Where the Stone had once stood there was now a deep, square depression in the earth, and in the center of that depression was a foaming, spouting, gushing fountain of water hundreds of feet high! The Stone had broken open a deep well, and now a mighty lake was forming, its waters not just filling the ditch, but overflowing it, filling the dips and low spots, flowing around the high spots, carrying water through the grasslands to the village and the crops.

The Motosas fell to their knees, raised their hands toward heaven, and sang to God.

"Look!" said Dr. Cooper, pointing below. "Nkromo's army!"

From their platform high on the smooth, flat face of the Stone, they could see hundreds of little dust clouds rising from the desert, kicked up by the feet, wheels, and tank tracks of the fleeing army—and the Stone was catching up.

"They're not going to make it!" Dr. Henderson cried, shaking her head.

"Look!" said Mobutu. "I see His Excellency!"

They searched in the direction Mobutu was pointing and finally spotted one tiny figure standing defiantly in the path of the Stone, one hand outstretched to point a silver saber, the other hand a shaking fist.

Mobutu shook his head in sorrow and wonder. "He still defies the Stone! He defies the God of the Motosas!"

The rolling, building mound of earth was tumbling toward the tiny little dictator with great speed, but he would not budge; he only stood there, a lonely little speck in the desert, shaking his fist in hate.

When the huge, mountainous wave of earth, stone, and sand rolled over Idi Nkromo, it only took an instant. First he was there, and then he was gone.

TWELVE

They sat on a mound of soft rubble: sand, dirt, small stones, bigger boulders. It was suddenly quiet—so suddenly that the Coopers, Dr. Henderson, Mr. Mobutu, and his two loyal sidekicks were the only things still shaking. The air started to clear up as the dust drifted away on a steady north breeze. The first question on everyone's mind was, *Where are we?*

They knew they were on solid, steady ground—at least, it wasn't rolling or tumbling. But they were up high, on a long range of hills they'd never seen before. To the east they could easily see the beginnings of green jungle and the white buildings of what had been called Nkromotown. But now that it was the capital of a small, free country no longer under the iron hand of a dictator, another name could be found.

To the west, they could see the largest, longest, deepest skid mark in the world, if not the known universe. The Stone had carved a deep, flat rut across the desert, and now, at the far end, an expansive lake was forming. The nation of Togwana would have to redraw its maps because it now had an entirely new geography: a vast lake where once there had been a desert and the hills upon which they sat that the Stone had scraped up.

Nkromo's army was gone. Some had perished with their boss under the moving mountain of earth. The rest had scattered into the jungles and small settlements to the east, no longer a powerful force now that their wicked leader was dead.

As the afternoon sun washed over the Coopers and their friends, they began to grasp the fact that the Stone was gone too. They could all remember the platform they were sitting on descending again, just like a plane coming in for a landing. They could remember the desert coming up to meet them, and they could even remember rolling gently off that platform onto this long, bulldozed pile of earth the Stone had created. But no one saw the moment the Stone vanished, and none could say just where it went. All they knew was it had done its work, left them here, and then disappeared as quickly as it had come.

Dr. Henderson was the first to speak. "Now that, my friends, was some kind of ride!"

Dr. Cooper was already on his knees. To pray his prayer of thanksgiving, all he had to do was remove his hat. "Lord, You have shown us that You are mighty indeed! But Your mercy is also as great as Your might, and for that, we thank You!"

"Do we ever," said Jay.

"Amen," said Lila.

"You're real, God," said Dr. Henderson. "You've gotten through to me. I believe."

148

Then they all sat there quietly, thoughtfully, pondering what had happened.

"Togwana will never be the same," said Mobutu, looking east and west. "We have a whole new country now."

"In more ways than one," said Dr. Cooper. "The geography is different, but you're also rid of Idi Nkromo. Now you and the rest of the people can rebuild Togwana the right way."

Mobutu nodded with understanding. "As God leads us. I have much to repent of. I have much to set right."

Dr. Cooper smiled at that. "No better time to start than right now, Mr. Mobutu."

"By the way," said Lila. "Thank you, Mr. Mobutu, for saving our lives."

"Yeah, thanks," Jay said, and then they all extended their thanks to Mr. Mobutu, Bernard, and Walter.

"Don't thank me," said Mobutu. "Thank your father. He knew."

Jay and Lila looked at their father. "Knew what?"

Dr. Cooper smiled at Mobutu. "Go ahead and tell them."

Mr. Mobutu sighed and then confessed, "I am a Motosa. Chief Gotono and I are from the same family, the Mobutus. We are cousins."

Lila's eyes got big, and then she slapped the ground with the realization. "So that's why you look so much alike!"

Mobutu nodded with a smile. "I grew up in the Motosa village. I knew of the Motosas' God."

"Remember the story of the Man in the Tree?" Dr. Cooper asked his kids and Dr. Henderson. "'God sent Ontolo to save Mobutu.' Mobutu was the chief's name before he became chief. I had a hunch there was a connection."

"And you guessed that I would fear God?" Mobutu asked.

Dr. Cooper eyed Mobutu knowingly. "I knew you did, somewhere deep in your heart."

Mobutu nodded. "My days among the Motosas were long ago, and I journeyed far from home to follow a man who was really a devil." He shook his head sorrowfully. "How thankful I am that God intervened and saved my people from Nkromo. How thankful I am that He saved *me!* Ontolo has saved Mobutu again—even when *this* Mobutu does not deserve it."

"Ontolo," Jay considered. "The Man in the Tree."

Mobutu smiled, nodding his head. "And a Stone the size of a mountain!"

"The same God, the same Savior," said Dr. Cooper.

But Dr. Henderson was still perplexed. "Well fine, Dr. Cooper, but that doesn't explain how you knew the rest."

He gave her a puzzled look. "What do you mean?"

She knew he was teasing her a bit. "Don't give me that! How did you know the Stone was going to, you know, grow, and move, and take out Idi Nkromo?"

Dr. Cooper raised an eyebrow, a twinkle in his eye. "Dare I refer to the Bible again?"

Dr. Henderson threw up her arms in surrender. "Go ahead, go ahead."

"All through the Bible you can find scriptures that compare Jesus to a stone or a rock: The rock in the wilderness that produced water when Moses struck it . . ." They all shot a glance at the lake still growing as water gushed out of the earth. "'And they all drank the same spiritual drink. They drank from that spiritual rock that was with them. That rock was Christ.' Oh, and then there's the rock upon which the wise man built his house . . ."

"And we saw how the Motosas used that idea," said Lila.

"Just like the stone the builders rejected that became the cornerstone. And then there's that scripture in Daniel . . ."

"Oh, yeah!" said Jay, recalling it.

Dr. Cooper explained. "When Daniel interprets a dream King Nebuchadnezzar had, he tells about a huge stone that was cut out without hands that smashed and destroyed all the evil kingdoms of the world, then grew into a mountain that filled the whole earth. It's a very exciting picture of Christ, and how He would eventually do away with the world's evil powers and fill it with His glory instead."

"I love it!" said Lila.

"So . . . since the Stone seemed to be God's way of showing the Motosas—and us—the power and majesty of Jesus Christ, I figured the Stone might act out that picture in the Book of Daniel."

Dr. Henderson cocked her head and raised an eyebrow. "Wasn't that kind of a long shot for a man about to *be* shot?"

"Well . . ." Dr. Cooper thought it over. "Considering everything else God has done to reveal Himself to the Motosas, it had to happen, and I knew Idi Nkromo couldn't last, not if the Motosas were to survive and Chief Gotono's dream was to come true."

That got their interest. "What dream?"

Weeks later, a small, single-engine airplane soared over Togwana's new lake and landed gently on the lake's western shore, only a quarter of a mile or so from the Motosa village. Green fields of wheat and corn flourished and sheep and goats drank their fill at the water's edge. The grasslands were greening up, and new homes were being built. Things had changed in Togwana.

As the plane taxied to a stop not far from the village, Brent Anderson, the once-exiled missionary, gazed out the window, drinking in the scene. "This is it, Jake! This is the village I wanted to reach! I know the Lord has called me here!"

Jacob Cooper shut down the engine and smiled at his friend. "I think they know it too. They've been expecting you for a long time."

Dr. Cooper, Brent Anderson, Jay, and Lila all stepped out of the plane while throngs of Motosas came running from the village, cheering and waving. It was a day the Motosas had been promised for years, and now it had finally arrived. Just as they had done for Dr. Henderson weeks ago, the warriors made chairs of their arms and bore all four of the visitors aloft, carrying them through the newly thriving grasslands, into the village, and into the big meeting hall where the rest of the villagers had already assembled.

The chief was standing on the large, square stone in front, ready to welcome them. Brent Anderson was brought right to the front, introduced to the chief, and then embraced by the powerful, jovial man dressed like a big bush. The Coopers took a bench over to the side where Bengati was waiting to interpret the proceedings for them.

The chief raised his big arms, and the crowd fell silent. Then he began to speak.

Bengati leaned close and interpreted for the Coopers. "You all know the dream our God gave me: That someday a man with blond hair would come down out of the sky and open the leaves he held in his hand," the chief made the gesture with his hands that symbolized the opening of a book, "and that the leaves would speak and tell us the name of our God. I never understood how leaves could speak, until my son . . ." The chief had to stop a moment to choke back tears as he looked down at Ontolo, who sat in the front row with paper and pencils he'd received from the Coopers, ready to write. "Until my son found a way with his little marks. Now, the leaves can speak. Now, the man from the sky with light hair has come!"

The crowd cheered. The Coopers cheered.

The chief continued, "You know that Jacob Cooper came to us from the sky with light hair and much wisdom, but he was not the man in my dream." Then the chief added with a twinkle in his eye, "But we were not wrong about Jacob Cooper and his children—they were just early!"

The people laughed.

The chief guided Brent Anderson onto the large speaking rock and said to the crowd, "Here is the man our God has promised!"

Brent Anderson, moved to the point of tears, took his big, black Bible, opened it, and began to read to them from the Gospel of John, interpreting the Scriptures directly into Motosan, a language he had already learned.

All over the building, people's faces glowed as they listened, looked at one another, and then made the opening book gesture with their hands. The leaves, they agreed, were now speaking.

"For years your God has spoken to you of Himself and His Son who came to earth to save you," Brent said in Motosan as Bengati interpreted for the Coopers. "He showed you through your stories how sin can bite like a snake and destroy you. He showed you through the Man in the Tree how He would provide someone who would take away the bite of the snake by taking sin's punishment upon Himself. According to your own story, He sent Ontolo to save Mobutu."

Dr. Cooper smiled quietly as he looked across the room and saw D. M. Mobutu, the new president-elect of Togwana, sitting next to Chief Gotono, his cousin. The new government and the Motosas had already established a friendly, working relationship.

Brent continued, "Finally, He showed you how this Man in the Tree would not remain a man in a tree, dying from the arrows and spears of sin, but would someday come to earth as a mighty mountain that would sweep evil from the earth, give us rest from our enemies, and water our lands."

Lila folded her arms as if she were cold. "Wow, this is giving me goosebumps!"

Jay pointed across the room. "Look at Ontolo."

Lila looked to see the chief's son writing down what Brent Anderson was saying, using his own alphabet.

"He wants to start writing out the Bible in Motosan," said Jay. "Looks like God thought of everything."

Brent turned a page in his Bible. The leaves continued to speak. "Because God so loved all people, He sent His Son to save not only Motosas, but all people. If we believe in His Son, we will not die, but will live forever with Him."

That got a cheer from the crowd. It was what they'd been waiting to hear for years.

"Even now, even today, the Man in the Tree, the one you call Ontolo, will save us and take us back into His arms. I have come to tell you about Him and to tell you His name."

There was a gasp from the crowd and even from the chief.

"The name of our God!" said Bengati in a hushed, excited voice. "We have waited so long. . . ."

"His name is Jesus," said Brent, "the Man in the Tree, who takes away the sins of the whole world."

Dr. Cooper wiped a tear from his eye. Jesus. The Man in the Tree. The Savior. The Stone the builders rejected. The Chief Cornerstone. The Stone that would someday destroy all wicked kings and fill the whole earth with His glory.

He had come at last to the Motosas.